DINOSAUR FEVER

Marion Woodson

A SANDCASTLE BOOK

A MEMBER OF THE DUNDURN GROUP
TORONTO

Editor: Michael Carroll
Design: Erin Mallory
Printer: Webcom

Library and Archives Canada Cataloguing in Publication

Woodson, Marion
    Dinosaur fever / Marion Woodson.

ISBN 978-1-55002-690-0

    I. Title.

PS8595.O653D55 2008   jC813'.54   C2007-900907-7

1   2   3   4   5   12   11   10   09   08

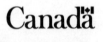

Conseil des Arts   Canada Council
du Canada   for the Arts

ONTARIO ARTS COUNCIL
CONSEIL DES ARTS DE L'ONTARIO

We acknowledge the support of **The Canada Council for the Arts** and the **Ontario Arts Council** for our publishing program. We also acknowledge the financial support of the **Government of Canada** through the **Book Publishing Industry Development Program** and **The Association for the Export of Canadian Books**, and the **Government of Ontario** through the **Ontario Book Publishers Tax Credit** program, and the **Ontario Media Development Corporation**.

Care has been taken to trace the ownership of copyright material used in this book. The author and the publisher welcome any information enabling them to rectify any references or credits in subsequent editions.

J. Kirk Howard, President

Printed and bound in Canada.
www.dundurn.com

Dundurn Press	Gazelle Book Services Limited	Dundurn Press
3 Church Street, Suite 500	White Cross Mills	2250 Military Road
Toronto, Ontario, Canada	High Town, Lancaster, England	Tonawanda, NY
M5E 1M2	LA1 4XS	U.S.A. 14150

For my grandsons:
Charles, Thomas, Sam, Jake, Alec, and Evan

ACKNOWLEDGEMENTS

Sunni Turner deserves much of the credit for supplying the background information for this novel, and also for her first-hand accounts of activities at a dinosaur dig. She was there! I also wish to thank Michael Carroll for diligent editing and for his good-humoured approachability.

PROLOGUE

The great animal guards her nest. Ten eggs are snug and warm under a blanket of rotting vegetation. She turns her head sideways and lowers her ear, listening for sound from inside the egg shells. It won't be long now — some of the nearby nests are already squirming with big-eyed, limp-bodied newborns.

She dozes in the warm sunshine. The air is pungent with the smell of conifer sap and animal sweat.

A long-legged birdlike creature darts in to steal an egg from her neighbour's unguarded nest, and the mother bellows with rage and thumps her tail. She hunches in a toad-like stance, her long, flat tail and her short forelegs resting on the ground. The muscles in her powerful hind legs ripple and bulge as she moves.

Suddenly alert, she stands. Something has changed! A huge column of black rises from a mountain on the horizon. The sky turns orange.

Above the usual trumpets and snorts of hundreds of her fellow creatures feeding, nesting, and foraging nearby she can hear a strange sound — a faint thunder-like reverberation. The noise grows louder. The earth trembles.

Deep within her consciousness the mother recognizes danger, but the menace is not familiar. She moves closer to her nest and uses her snout to nudge the leaves and twigs over the eggs, then raises her head and swivels her slender neck slowly. Her huge eyes in outwardly projecting sockets scan the landscape in every direction. Nothing seems out of place — only the changing colour of the sky, the rumbling noise, and the slight tremors of the earth.

Other animals are on the alert now. Heads are up. For a moment all is silent except for the squeaks and cries of hungry hatchlings. The ground shakes, but the mud nest holds the eggs securely in place. Rolling booms intermingle with the warning cries of animals. A gust of wind carries the smell of sulphur.

CHAPTER 1

Adam Zapotica knew the moment he saw the newspaper headline and article that he had to go:

DINOSAUR NESTS FOUND ON ALBERTA'S MILK RIVER RIDGE

Paleontologists have begun work on one of the most important discoveries in fifty years — seven clutches of *Hadrosaur* eggs containing perfectly preserved articulated dinosaur embryos. The eggs have been tentatively identified as those of the crested duckbill, *Hypacrosaurus*. These animals appear to have been nurturing parents. There is evidence that the young of the species were guarded and fed by the adults for several months after incubation.

It was the most exciting project he could imagine: excavating nests made seventy-five million years ago by three-tonne duckbill dinosaurs. Incredibly, the egg-filled nests were in situ — in exactly the same place as when they were built. These weren't the first eggs to be found in North America — a major nesting area had been uncovered in Montana just a year or two earlier — but these were the best because of the articulated embryos. Tiny bones and teeth and claws and tails were still connected.

So he had to go.

There were some problems, though. Number one: volunteers at dinosaur digs had to be at least eighteen years old, and he was only fifteen. Number two: he had a part-time job stocking shelves at the local drugstore. Number three: it was a two-day, three-hundred-kilometre bicycle ride from Calgary to Devil's Coulee. And number four: his parents might veto the idea.

He was pretty sure he could handle all of the problems except number one. He could trade working hours with the other part-time drugstore employee, he could work out at the gym to get in shape for the ride and arrange an overnight stop at his aunt's house in Vulcan, and he could probably convince his parents that experience at a dinosaur dig would look great on his résumé when he was hunting for summer jobs to get himself through university.

That still left problem number one. He wasn't old enough. Period. And even if he were the right age, the odds against him succeeding were probably about the same as those of winning a lottery. Getting permission to go in just because he wanted to see the dinosaur eggs? Who was he kidding? There were probably thousands of people who wanted to see them, but he *had* to try.

Adam tracked down Dr. James Lawson, a paleontologist who had supervised a school work experience project he'd done on the dinosaur display at the Calgary Zoo two years earlier. Lawson gave him a letter of reference, though he didn't think it would "cut much ice," as he put it. But the recommendation was better than nothing, and with it in hand, Adam started off in high spirits.

By the afternoon of the second day of his bicycle trip, Adam was beginning to question his sanity. Curse the dust, curse the sweltering heat, curse the relentless wind, and curse the Sunday drivers! Three times in forty minutes he'd had to stop, take out his contact lenses, suck the dust off them, and pray that the howling gale wouldn't snatch them off his finger before he managed to get them back into place.

There was only one thing to do. He would have to wear his regular glasses with the snap-on shades. Adam hated the way he looked in the thick glasses — like an owlish nerd a couple of pounds short of a bushel — but he'd never get to his destination at this rate. He needed a rest, a drink of water, and a peek at the map. There was a gully just ahead and a large culvert under the road. The end of the culvert was pretty depressing — littered with plastic bags, Styrofoam cups, and candy wrappers — but it was sheltered from the sun and wind and was quiet except when a vehicle thundered overhead.

Adam crawled in, took his lenses out, squirted lukewarm water into his parched mouth, put on his glasses, then lay back in the dust with his head on his pack and studied the map. He had just passed Monarch, which meant he still had another seventeen kilometres to go until he reached Lethbridge, then another thirty to Raymond, twenty-eight to Warner, and he would be practically there. Adam had cycled ninety-seven kilometres since seven o'clock that morning. It was two o'clock in the afternoon, and he still had seventy-five to go!

How could he have been such an idiot, wasting his time and energy like this? It was crazier than imagining he could get up onstage and be a rock star. The people in charge at the dig probably wouldn't even give him the time of day, never mind an invitation into their private world.

Still, he had come this far. "Best foot forward," he muttered with a groan.

All he could glimpse through the round porthole end of the culvert was sorry-looking pastureland with a lot of eroded patches and hills and gullies. Here and there in the sparse grasslands prickly pear and wild honeysuckle grew. The desert scent of sagebrush permeated the wind. The countryside he was in was the perfect habitat for rattlesnakes, black widow spiders, and scorpions. He shivered and checked himself for anything that crawled. Then he stood, tucked his paraphernalia into his pack, lifted his bicycle, and climbed back to the road.

It was 6:20 p.m. when Adam got stiffly off his bike in Warner to ask directions of a man who was getting out of the cab of a tractor-trailer truck parked beside a café.

"Twenty-eight kilometres to the turnoff — dirt road going across a field," the truck driver said. "Big farm owned by Hutterites. Black Angus cattle — a granary in the distance."

Adam used the café pay phone to call home collect and told his mother he was there, or at least pretty close. By 7:23 he could see the cattle, the granary, the dirt road, a newish barbed-wire fence, and a chain-link gate. Closed. Padlocked.

He wheeled his bike into the ditch and dropped it. Sitting on the low bank, he flopped back onto the grass and stared at the sky. So was this it — locked out without a single human being in sight? What now? He couldn't stand the thought of getting on that lousy bike and heading home. His stomach was tied in knots and his head felt as if it were stuffed with old socks.

Singing? Was that singing he could hear? Adam jumped to his feet and held his breath. There it was again! He could see the singer now, straightening up from a crouched position on the other side of the fence and examining something in her hand.

"Hey, there!" he called. "Wait a second, will you?"

She turned and stared at him. "Who are you?" She walked toward the gate. Her dark hair, falling loose from one big braid at the back of her head, was silver-grey with dust and her cheeks and nostrils and the corners of her mouth were streaked black. She wore dark-rimmed glasses and carried a white canvas bag with a drawstring and the words ALBERTA GOVERNMENT printed on the side.

Adam realized he was gawking. He glanced away, then back at her. "I'm Adam. Pleased to meet you, um, what did you say your name was?"

"I didn't say, and what are you doing here? This is a high-security area. Are you with the press or TV, because if you are, you might as well bug off. Nobody's allowed past that gate without credentials." She slipped her wrist through the drawstring of her bag, put her fists on her hips, and studied him intently.

Adam figured she was probably no more impressed with his appearance than he was with hers. His only hope was persuasion. "I'm not *with* anybody, unless you count mosquitoes and horseflies. I've been on my bike for —" he shrugged "— it seems like a couple of hundred years. All I want to do is see the dinosaur nests. Just see them, that's all. I've got a letter of reference from Dr. James Lawson. He works at the Royal Tyrrell Museum in Drumheller."

"My, I'm impressed!" the girl said with a playful smile. "You're still not going to get in."

"Darn!" he muttered gloomily. "Oh, well, I guess this trip's not a total waste. Maybe I'll go home and write a travel article — 'Roadside Ditches Between Calgary and the Milk River Ridge: Explore the Fascinating Habits of the Litterbug.'"

"Complete with a 'Not to be Missed List,' I suppose? Things like pepperoni pizza crusts, watermelon rinds, plastic baby bottle liners …" She smiled again. Her teeth were very white framed in that grimy face.

"You got it! I could draw all that. That's why I want into the dig, so I can draw it."

"You draw? With a pencil or something?" She raised one hand and made drawing motions in the air with her thumb and forefinger.

He nodded.

"What kind of stuff do you draw usually?"

"Dinosaurs." He kicked at the ground. "But I guess it was a crazy dream to think I might get to see the nests and make some sketches." He shook his head angrily. "I'll just get going then …" He stared dejectedly at a meadowlark singing its flutelike tune from a fencepost. Dumb bird! Wasting its energy trying to sound cheerful in the dust-bowl capital of the world.

"Wait a minute," she said. "Let's see the letter."

He shoved it through the gate, and she read it quickly.

"How do I know this is for real? Where's your art stuff?"

"In my pack. I'll get it. Don't go away." Maybe there was some hope, after all. If only she liked his sketches …

"Don't rush," she said. "It's too hot." She swung the canvas bag back and forth slowly.

Adam unzipped a clear plastic case, pulled out his pad,

and held it up so she could see as he turned the pages, holding them gingerly at the corners.

"Yeah," the girl said with a nod. "You do draw. Watch out, though! Don't get them dirty."

Adam slipped the pad back into the case, then flipped up his sunglass shades and peered through his thick lenses without even thinking about looking like a nerd. The girl wore heavy grey knit socks, hiking boots, denim shorts, and a long-sleeved khaki shirt. Around her waist was a belt with various weird tools attached to it. She jingled and clattered as she moved, and puffs of dust seemed to surround her like Pigpen in the *Peanuts* comic strip.

At the same time she was quite obviously sizing him up, and Adam wondered what she was thinking. She wouldn't call him handsome or a "hunk" — that was for sure. He wasn't very tall, 1.7 metres, to be precise, and he was heavy-set. His legs and arms were muscular, his face was round, and he had thick blond eyebrows that grew right across the bridge of his nose. His eyes were hazel. He liked his hair. It shone reddish-blond in the sunlight, had a slight natural curl, and was very thick and coarse, so he always felt a little taller when it was freshly shampooed.

Oh, and the freckles! His arms, legs, and face swarmed with freckles that hatched in the sunshine like mosquito larvae.

The girl was staring at the ground, obviously thinking hard. "Maybe I could get you in. Just for a day or so," she said, the frown of concentration on her forehead accentuated by streaks of dust.

"You think so?" A burst of energy flooded Adam. "I'd give anything. I'd appreciate it forever. Honest I would."

The canvas bag clunked dully against the gate as the girl reached up and hooked her fingers through the chain-link.

"Yeah. My dad's in charge here. Of course, I might have to tell a little white lie …" Her face was animated now. "What's your name again?"

"Adam Zapotica. What's yours?"

"Jamie Jamieson, and our first problem is to get your bike through the fence. Go down into that gully.

He walked the bike to where she indicated, and she met him on the other side of the fence.

You're not eighteen, are you?" she asked with a grunt. She was kneeling, trying to hold the front wheel of the bicycle straight and lift and pull at the same time. "Nobody under eighteen is allowed to be here, you know." She acted as if she were explaining something to a five-year-old.

Adam tried to look indignant. "You think I don't know that? Yeah, I'm not eighteen, but I'll be … uh … seventeen in January." He hated fibbing, but what else could he do? "Just how old are you, anyway?"

"Sixteen." She sat back with a thump as the bike became unstuck and lunged toward her.

"Sorry about that," Adam said. "How come you're here then if you're only sixteen?"

"My dad's the preparator. I've been dragged to dinosaur digs since I was four years old."

Poor you, Adam thought. He would have given anything to be dragged to even one dig.

"Come on," she said, "let's go introduce you to my dad." Then she turned with a jingle and a hop, and Adam followed.

CHAPTER 2

As Adam and Jamie walked toward the camp, he saw various kinds of accommodations huddled in a shallow valley.

"Where do you plan to sleep?" Jamie asked, scrutinizing his pack, which obviously didn't hold a tent.

"Under the wide and starry. I've got a sleeping bag."

"If Dad will let you stay, maybe you could use Norm's place. He got a fever and had to go home. We aren't sure if it's a spider bite or what." She headed in the direction of a big trailer.

"You seem pretty sure you can square it with your father." Adam was worried. Okay, she was the boss's daughter and she was pretty sure of herself. In fact, bossy might be a better word. But still ...

"Trust me," she told him as she stepped through the open door of the trailer.

Two long tables littered with fossilized bones marked with numbers and letters stretched along the entire length of the trailer. Some of the bones were wrapped in burlap and covered with plaster of Paris, but many looked as if they had been varnished.

"Hi, Dad," Jamie said.

A man carrying a clipboard was bent over one of the tables. "It's about time you got back, Jamie. And who have you got there?" He peered at Adam suspiciously.

"This is Adam. He's a professional artist and he's got a

letter from a Dr. Lawson recommending him to come and do artwork for us."

A *professional* artist? Adam thought. Where did she get that from? He had never sold a painting in his life. Adam squelched the small voice of conscience trying to be heard. It wasn't going to matter, anyway.

Mr. Jamieson shook his head. "Jamie, honey, you know the rules. We can't make exceptions, or we'll have them crawling out of the woodwork."

"Aw, come on, Dad. He's an old friend of mine."

Adam frowned. Another one of her little white lies. He stared at a hollow-eyed skull on the table.

"Oh? I've never heard you mention a friend named Adam."

"You haven't?" She sounded genuinely surprised. "I met him at the Banff School of Fine Arts when I was doing that course there. Adam, why don't you show my dad the letter and your drawings?"

She smiled at him in what she probably intended to be an "old friend" kind of way, but to Adam it seemed about as genuine as the expression on a toothpaste ad model.

"Hmm," Mr. Jamieson said as he read the letter. "Not bad," he added as he examined the drawings. He glanced at Jamie, then at Adam, then back at Jamie. "Well, I guess we'll take a chance just this once. You're absolutely certain you can vouch for him?"

"Absolutely," she said.

"All right. See to it he understands all the ground rules." Mr. Jamieson offered his hand to Adam. "I'm Al."

Adam rubbed the palm of his right hand on his jeans. "Uh, I'm pretty grubby."

"It's okay, son. No one can keep clean long around

here." Mr. Jamieson was clean. He was freshly shaven, his dark greying hair was short, and his beige cotton pants and white short-sleeved shirt appeared as if they had just come from the laundry. His dark-rimmed glasses magnified his light grey eyes.

Adam was overwhelmed. Here he was smack in the middle of dinosaur bones, and he could stay! There were a few misconceptions that had to be cleared up, but he would worry about that later. "Pardon?" he said when he realized Jamie was asking him something. "Sorry. My thoughts were wandering."

"Have you had supper?"

Adam shook his head. "Are there any eggs in here?"

"No. Were you thinking scrambled or fried?" Mr. Jamieson chuckled and made a flipping motion with his clipboard.

Adam grinned. "No, I was thinking of whipping up a marble cake." Things were looking better, Adam mused. Mr. Jamieson had a sense of humour. He was okay.

"No, seriously, son, we haven't got any dinosaur eggs out yet. It takes a long time to prepare the site. We've taken off the overburden, marked the locations, and actually started on two of the nests. What are you up to now, Jamie? Find anything interesting?"

Jamie was taking bits and pieces from her canvas bag — they looked like a collection of rough little rocks that could be picked up on any roadside. "Not sure what this is." She held one of the bits close to her face and squinted at it. "But I found another tooth."

"You did? You're a real bird dog when it comes to teeth." Mr. Jamieson glanced at Adam. "Jamie's on the trail of *T. rex*, so to speak. She's found a few teeth, yet there's no evidence the big guys actually lived here. We haven't found any trace of skeletons, so …" He shrugged. "Maybe they were just passing through and stopped for lunch." He made his voice deep and gruff. "I'll have a *Euoplocephalus* steak and a side order of deep-fried *Ornithomimus* wings, please."

Adam stretched his head back to gaze at the ceiling, then pretended to write on the palm of his hand. "And how would you like that steak, sir?"

They all laughed, and Mr. Jamieson slapped Adam's back.

"So when do you think you'll actually get eggs out of the nests?" Adam asked, trying to make his voice sound natural, though his heart was beating faster than usual.

"What do you think, Jamie?"

"Probably tomorrow, Dad. With any luck."

"Yeah. I'd guess tomorrow. But mum's the word." Mr. Jamieson regarded Adam sternly. "We'd like to keep the media people away until we're ready for them."

"Do you think Adam could stay in Norm's place?" Jamie asked. "He was going to sleep outside."

"Sure thing," her father said.

"Thanks," Adam said as Jamie led him through the camp. "I can't believe this is actually happening. The only thing is …"

"Yeah?"

"Well, for one thing, I'm not a professional anything."

"Your paintings look professional to me."

"Maybe, but that's not the generally accepted meaning of the word. And what about this 'old friend' business? How do I handle that?"

"Don't worry. You can fake it."

"Fake it? I know nothing about you. Zilch. Zero. I'll

make a fool of myself."

"Listen." She stopped and turned toward him. "I thought it was worth going to bat for you because it was something you seemed to want so badly. The odds were a thousand to one against you, so I stuck my neck out. Would you rather take a chance of making a fool of yourself or leave right now?"

Adam was contrite. She *had* stuck her neck out for him. "Sorry. You vouched for me and that's the only reason I'm here and I do appreciate it. What can I say?" He put his hand on her arm.

"It's okay. Actually, I do have an ulterior motive. I thought it would be fun to have somebody my own age around. The people are great, don't get me wrong, but they're older and a bit, um, stodgy. Know what I mean?"

"Yeah, stodgy," Adam said. So he better be the opposite of stodgy, he thought. What would that be? Interesting, exciting, stimulating? Good luck!

Jamie changed the subject. "I'm on my way for a shower. Guess you'd like one, too?"

"A shower? Yeah. A shower would be great."

"Norm's Place" looked like heaven. It was a rusty old camper meant to be sitting on the back of a pickup truck, but here it sat on the ground at the edge of the camp. Its licence plate said: ALBERTA. WILD ROSE COUNTRY. 1988.

"Thanks, Norm, wherever you are," Adam said as Jamie opened the door.

"It's not Norm's really. It's my dad's, but now he uses the Prowler and lets the graduate students use this."

"Thanks, then, to your dad. It looks great to me after two days on that bike." Adam dumped his pack onto the fold-down table.

"Come on," Jamie said, "I'll show you where the shower is and then I'll go see if the cook has any leftovers."

The "shower" was in a little grove of trees about a hundred metres along a winding path past Norm's place. It consisted of a truck inner tube filled with water set on a wooden framework. There were pieces of an old tarpaulin on three sides for semi-privacy and several chunks of flat shale for a floor.

At the end of the path four outdoor toilet stalls under one roof were separated by two-metre-high partitions.

"You can use half of what's left," Jamie said, pointing at the shower. "They'll fill it up again in the morning."

Half of what was left was about one-twentieth of the water Adam used at home at least once a day, but it was warm and it was wet.

He sat outside his new home in the only movable piece of furniture he could find — a slightly twisted aluminum folding chair. Adam was more or less clean. His glasses were off, his contact lenses were in, his stomach was full — Jamie had handed him a plateful of roast beef sandwiches before she'd gone for her own shower — and he had his sketchbook on his knee and a pencil behind his ear. And as an added bonus, the wind had subsided.

He stretched and laced his fingers behind his neck. The prairie scene at twilight was truly something. Mountains purpled the horizon, with the fainter outline of Devil's Coulee close by. That was where the nests were, and tomorrow he would actually see a dinosaur egg!

Yeah, dinosaur egg. And he was the *professional* artist. They would be expecting big things of him. He was setting himself up for a major embarrassment.

Exactly what did a *Hypacrosaurus* look like? Sure, he

could draw his impression of one, but would it satisfy the experts around here? They knew. He would probably get some detail horribly wrong, and they'd all laugh at him.

Adam decided he had to forget about dinosaurs and draw what he saw, so he began to sketch. The colours were so soft and spellbinding that he was glad he hadn't brought his pastels — he would never be able to capture those subtle hues on paper. A pink-and-golden haze transformed everything with a delicate glow. Tents, water barrels, bicycles, a dusty Jeep, makeshift clotheslines — all seemed ethereal, impossible to capture. He turned the page and started to draw the landscape the way it had appeared when the dinosaurs were here.

Intermittently, over vast periods of time, mountains heave and grow, spewing enormous quantities of dust and rubble into the air. The debris settles, and streams and rivers overflow as they carry it toward the sea, depositing sand and mud on the flat flood plains. The sea grows and shrinks over the millennia. Streams widen, join other streams, form meandering rivers bordered by swamps.

The land becomes dotted with ponds and green with vegetation. Dense forests of giant conifers — swamp cypress, redwood, sequoia, and china fir — block out the sun. Lush mosses and ferns are everywhere. Palm-like plants and katsura trees grow on the higher ground, some covered with vines — wild grape, monseed, and green briar. Myrtle, sweetleaf, box prothea, and poison ivy also find a niche.

These 932,000 hectares of rich river delta between the Rocky Mountains and the Bear Paw Sea are a haven for dinosaurs. Hundreds of thousands of duckbills feed on evergreens, dogwoods, and berry bushes. Other vegetarians — the armour-plated Ankylosaurs *the three-horned, six-tonne* Triceratops, *the thick-headed* Pachycephalosaurs — *graze, along with the duckbills, at different levels in the rich greenery, providing a takeout diner for the carnivores. Some of the herbivores are a lot easier to take out than others, though.*

The Ankylosaurus *can crouch under thick, spiky armour plating, or deliver fatal blows with its clubbed tail; the* Triceratops *can set even the largest predator reeling with its 1.2-metre-long horns; and the swift-running* Hypsilophodon *can outrace any pursuer. But the duckbills are not fast runners. Many of the old, the unwary, the young, and the sick die violently, prey to hungry raptors.*

Adam drew water lilies with kidney-shaped leaves floating on still water. On the shoreline he added thick rushes, tall horsetail, swamp grass, and moss. Behind this he outlined trees — vine-entwined sycamores, redwood, poplar, dogwood — then started on flowers and hesitated. What kind of flowers? There was no grass then, but he was sure there should be flowers on some of the trees. He leaned back and imagined insects darting around — a kind of giant dragonfly would be right at home, and probably some kind of bees.

"Hi! How you doing?" It was Jamie. A very different Jamie. Her damp hair, out of its braid, hung down her back in kinky waves, and her face was so scrubbed and rosy that it looked polished. She wore clean shorts, white running shoes with no laces, and an only slightly wrinkled navy blue T-shirt.

"Oh, hi, uh, ah …" Adam was momentarily unable to collect his thoughts, let alone form words.

"Wow, that's neat." Jamie glanced at his drawing. "It probably did look like that way back when. You look different." She tilted her head and studied him. "I've got contacts, too, but I don't use them out here. Too much hassle trying to keep the dust out of my eyes."

Her eyes were startlingly bright in her tanned face. Green or blue? he wondered. Or a mixture of both? "Really?" he finally said, swallowing. "I guess I won't wear mine, either, when we go up to the dig."

"There's no alcohol allowed and no radios. And your hair's the wrong length." She nodded knowingly. "It'll be in your eyes all day and will drive you crazy."

"It is? Well, pardon *me*!" He felt like a disobedient child, sitting here with this bespectacled young *person* giving him a lecture about what he should and shouldn't do. Even how to wear his hair! But he'd better watch his step. He was the stranger in a new situation, and she was his only ally. "Yeah, I guess you're right," he said in a conciliatory tone. "So what if people start asking questions about this 'old friend' business?"

"Don't worry. I'll be there to coach you." She smiled and winked, and if Adam hadn't been so nervous, he would have winked back.

Not being stodgy was going to take practice.

CHAPTER 3

Several people were gathered around a campfire, some standing, others sitting at picnic tables.

"This is Adam," Jamie announced. "He's an old friend of mine and a terrific artist. He draws dinosaurs like you wouldn't believe."

"Hi," Adam said.

The others looked up, called greetings, waved.

A young woman was seated at a table. "This is Bonnie," Jamie said. "Bonnie, meet Adam."

"Hi, sweetie. Welcome to Digsville." Bonnie waved two fingers, sized Adam up, probably decided he was too young, or too short, or too something, and called to Jamie's father. "Al, while you're up, would you bring me a little drink of something. Maybe orange juice? There's a pet."

Bonnie was a paleontology student at the University of Alberta in Edmonton. She wore cowboy boots and a knee-length smock over cotton leggings. Her hair was tied back in a ponytail with a bright pink silk scarf.

"This is Kanga and Baby Roo," she said as she picked up a large stuffed kangaroo with a baby in its pouch and hugged it to her chest. "Aren't they adorable? My sweetie-pie uncle brought them back from Australia. He always brings me nice things. Doesn't he, Kanga?" She kissed the top of the furry head.

"Here's your drink, Bonnie girl." Mr. Jamieson set a glass in front of her.

This was a pretty democratic group, Adam thought. Al was the only paid person here. As well as supervising the field work, the preparator had to put it all together after the digging was done — make skeletons out of bits and pieces of bones. And he seemed perfectly willing to get Bonnie drinks.

A man who was sitting on the end of a table started to strum a ukulele and sing a song about a woman named Bobby McGee. A cowboy at a dinosaur dig? He certainly looked and acted like a cowboy. Talked like one, too. Even had a cowboy name.

"That's Slim Hardisty," Jamie said.

Small wrinkles fanned out around Slim's eyes, giving him a squinty look. He seemed about fifty years old. His horses were called Old Spike and Giddyup. Slim talked about his horses and his wife. Giddyup's name was really Napoleon, but he wasn't the fastest thing on four legs and it was a lot easier to say "Giddyup" and be done with it than yell "Giddyup, Napoleon."

Slim's wife got three and a half a day. "Three meals and half a bed," he explained, and everybody laughed.

His wife *looked* like a cowgirl — fringed shirt, white straw Stetson hat, cowboy boots — but she didn't speak like one. She talked like a paleontologist — about the Judith River Formation and fossil fauna and habitat influenced by rising western mountains. Her name was Denise. "Have you known our Jamie long?" she asked.

Adam's palms began to sweat, and he felt a tightening of his jaw. "Um, not too —"

"We were at the Banff School together last spring," Jamie interjected quickly. "Come and meet Sy." She pulled Adam away.

Sy was older. A lot older — seventy-five at least. Both

his first and last names began with an *S* and had a lot of consonants and not many vowels. He was tall and thin-faced and wore a green cotton work shirt and a Panama hat. Adam expected him to say, "Dr. Livingstone, I presume?" as he reached out to shake hands. What he did say was: "Just call me Sy."

Sy crossed his legs, clasped his hands around one knee, and commenced to tell the story of his life, or so it seemed to Adam. He was a retired geologist and had done a lot of exploring in "the oil patch" for one of the big companies. That was how he'd become interested in fossils and artifacts.

"Sy has enough old bones to start his own museum," Jamie said.

"Have a care now," Sy said with a grin. "Just be careful what you say about my bones."

Slim sang a song about staying around and playing some old town too long, and Adam wasn't sorry when Mr. Jamieson said, "I think I've stayed around and played around this campfire long enough. Good-night, all." He left, and the others followed.

Adam decided it was worth the trouble of lowering the camper table level with the two side benches to form a bed, rather than sleeping in the low space over where the truck cab should be. What luxury! He could see a few stars through the open overhead vent and part of the Big Dipper through the side window.

He was here. On the inside of the fence. And he could stay ... for a while, anyway. The people seemed nice enough, so why wasn't he feeling exultant, elated, thrilled? Was it because all his planning, hoping, and working toward the moment had been so intense that a letdown was inevitable? Was it because he was worried about his artwork measuring up, or doing or saying something stupid in his role as an "old friend" of Jamie's? Was it because he didn't know how to avoid being stodgy? How could he possibly hope to turn into Mr. Personality all of a sudden?

Things looked brighter in the light of early dawn.

"Digsville," as Bonnie had called it, boasted tents, trailers, campers, a couple of trucks, a Jeep, an old Volkswagen Beetle, and several bicycles.

An Atco trailer served as a cookhouse/dining room, and that was where Adam was heading when he heard running footsteps behind him and felt a slap on the back.

"Hi, guy! Put her there, man! Mike's the name, micropaleo's the game." An exuberant young man with longish dark hair tied back with an elastic band clasped Adam's hand and shook it vigorously.

"Micropaleontology?" Adam said. "So you study the —"

"Yeah. The micro sites, the little guys — frogs, bugs."

"Uh … nice to meet you."

"Ditto." Mike scrutinized Adam with a puzzled frown. "So you're the famous artist. I thought you'd be older. Anyway, catch you later." He headed in the direction of the toilets on the run.

The activity in the cookhouse reminded Adam of a large family of kids getting ready for school. People were eating, slapping lunches together, grabbing fruit and juice boxes from the fridge, sorting through water canteens in the freezer, and looking for misplaced backpacks.

A young man who reminded Adam of Mike, except he was blond with short hair, paused with a cup of coffee in one hand and a slice of toast in the other. "Hi, I'm Hans. You must be …?"

"Adam. Nice to meet you."

Hans balanced the toast on his coffee cup and offered his left hand for a shake.

"You from around here?" Adam asked. He had decided to try to keep all conversation focused on other people.

"No. University of British Columbia. Excuse for a second. I better grab something for lunch."

"Hans is a sedimentologist," Jamie said. She was kneeling on the floor, fitting food and drink around various tools in her pack. "He's working on a thesis with a long name — about rocks."

Adam didn't have much difficulty fitting lunch around his supplies — two sketchbooks, twelve pencils in a case, and a small pencil sharpener. He was just closing the door of the camper, ready to leave with the others, when Bonnie came running across the road with a camera.

"Hold it, sweetie. I need a picture for my album. Smile! Say 'sex'! Gotcha!"

At 6:30 a.m. a party of ten set out for the dig. Cowboy Slim didn't go. His role, as far as Adam could see, was to provide support for his wife, amuse and entertain with stories and song, and be the gofer — take the water barrels to Warner and fill them up every second day, run into Raymond for groceries, make an overnight trip into Calgary for glyptal, a preservative, and plaster of Paris.

In addition to the people Adam had already met — Mr. Jamieson, Jamie, Bonnie, Denise, Sy, Mike, and Hans — there were two new faces.

"You must be Adam. I'm Lois." A short-haired, healthy-looking woman of about forty transferred a pencil from her right hand to her left, which held a notebook, and shook his hand. She and Denise walked together, and Adam overheard snatches of conversation about rose mallows, brown-eyed susans, and sunflowers. They seemed to be absorbed in identifying wildflowers and plants.

"Hi, there! Welcome aboard. I'm Herbie." A small dark young man fell into step beside Adam.

"Thanks. I'm Adam. Are you from around here?"

"Yes, from the University of Alberta."

"Paleontologist?" Adam asked.

"Uh-huh. I'm working on the digestive systems." He had a slight lisp and pronounced the words *digethtive thythtems*. "I classify coprolites."

Adam looked puzzled.

"Droppings," Herbie said.

"Oh …"

"I understand you're going to be our resident artist for a few days." Herbie bent down, picked up a stone, and turned it over. "Do you do book illustrations or gallery work or what?"

Adam tried to make his face appear normal, but his lips felt tight as he shook his head. "Not really. Mostly just private stuff."

Jamie, the rescuer, had apparently overheard, because she immediately joined them. "Watch your step as we climb the hill," she warned. "The caliche can be tricky if you step on it the wrong way."

"Caliche?" Adam asked.

"Yeah," Jamie said. "The little white stones. They can send you skidding along the sandstone on your butt quicker than you can say calcium carbonate."

"Or into a cactus," Herbie added. "And that's not an adventure without peril."

Adam grimaced. "I guess."

The countryside was stark and inhospitable. Great expanses of prairie grasses — spear grass and wheat grass — were interrupted by eroded patches of rock and dirt. A few oil well pumps bobbed their grasshopper heads up and down, up and down. The morning sky was clear, and the wind hadn't started to prowl yet. On the dry southern slope of Devil's Coulee grew prickly pear, cushion cactus, sagebrush, yellow violets, and prairie onion.

"John Palliser sure got it right two hundred years ago when he said this country wasn't fit for human habitation," Adam said.

"Oh, like really? Did he say that?" Jamie gazed around. "I guess it does seem kind of barren, but I like it." She put her hands behind her back and shoved her pack higher.

"Oh, yeah, it's nice in a way," Adam said quickly. Actually, the ambience was improving. There were surprises in the sear landscape — patches of bright yellow buffalo beans, golden asters, bluebells. Ground squirrels popped beady-eyed heads out of dens, peered around with quick movements, then crept cautiously out to sit up straight and swivel their necks to search for danger.

"Isn't it just the most perfect thing?" Jamie shaded her eyes with a hand and gazed up at the coulee. "Only a tiny fraction of dinosaur remains are ever fossilized and here we have whole nests right in our own backyard."

Adam tried to think of something un-stodgy to say. "Yeah, funny, isn't it? All this time they've been finding fossils of adults but no kids. They just weren't looking in the right place. I mean — right church, wrong pew."

"You got it," Jamie said. "The duckbills laid their eggs in upper coastal plains where there was good mud-pie stuff for nests."

"And I think the most amazing thing of all is that they cared for their young." Mr. Jamieson had joined them. "Evidence from the Montana site indicates the little guys were fed by one or both parents for several months."

"So they weren't the big clumsy lummoxes we've been led to believe," Adam said. "I always suspected as much."

"Right, Mr. Einstein," Jamie said with a teasing smile.

On the northern slope of the coulee there were larger shrubs and a few trees. Saskatoon bushes hung with purple berries, wild roses stored the sun in rosy hips, buckbrush and kinnikinnick spread thick branches over the ground.

"Listen …" Jamie said. "That's why radios are banned. So we can hear the birds."

Mourning doves cooed, and horned larks added clear, high-pitched voices from overhead.

As they climbed the bare sandstone bluff, Mr. Jamieson stopped to point out bones and parts of eggs eroding out of the hillside.

"Wow! That's incredible!" Adam said, crouching beside Jamie's father. "They're sure hard to see."

This fossil-hunting business wasn't as easy as it sounded. There were no signs saying BABY BONES HERE, and no pointing arrows stating FOSSILS THIS WAY.

"Here's the femur from a baby dinosaur," Jamie said, pointing at a tiny stick protruding from the rock. It was less than two centimetres long. "The same leg bone in an adult would be over a metre long. Pretty small babies for such big animals, eh?"

Adam whistled. "Yeah, really."

The wind had started to blow again, and his hair *was* the wrong length. He hated to admit it, but Jamie was right. Everybody, men and women, wore their hair very short or tied back in a braid or ponytail.

He must look like one of those plastic troll dolls his little sister collected. He wore shorts, gym shoes, and a T-shirt. His orangey freckled face, legs, and arms were slathered with sunscreen; his reddish hair spiked around his head like cushion cactus; and he peered through his double layer of eyeglasses like a squinty-eyed mole.

Adam forgot whipping hair, whirling dust, and squinty eyes in the excitement of actually seeing the nests and the eggs, flattened like fat pancakes from millions of years under pressure. They were the size of pie plates and were arranged in a herringbone pattern in circles in their rock beds. His skin crawled, and he felt a deep yearning to know and understand the creature that had built this nest. He touched one of the eggs, running his fingers over the pebbly surface.

Mr. Jamieson was watching. "Pretty thrilling stuff, isn't it?"

Adam nodded.

Devil's Coulee rose in bumps and ridges at a steep incline, and two flat ledges had been cut into the side hill, providing platforms for the workers. Around the platforms two-sided screens made of metal posts and fine black nylon webbing protected them from the wind and dust coming from the south and west. They also helped keep the nests free of soil buildup.

Jamie, along with Bonnie, Herbie, and Denise, gathered around one of the sites and began to unpack tools: geology hammers, knives, chisels, paintbrushes, whisk brooms, medicine droppers, small dental picks, ice picks, toothbrushes, even a mascara brush. They also each produced a field notebook, a bottle of glyptal, and empty medicine vials for bits of egg shell and other small finds. Then they began to work, two people on one egg, chipping and brushing with meticulous care.

The other group — Lois, Sy, and Hans — had moved to a different site about eight metres away.

"The animals were seven to ten metres long, and that was sort of the pecking distance," Jamie said. "They had togetherness and still had room to move around. You don't need other people looking over your shoulder when you're trying to get your nest just right, now do you?"

"I guess not," Adam said.

Mike was huddled over his micro site farther up the hill where two wind-eroded hoodoos punctured the skyline. Mr. Jamieson, with his map on a metal clipboard, was as excited as an expectant father, moving from one group to the other, giving instructions and encouragement.

Denise was the fossil illustrator. The site had been marked out with string and stakes into a grid. She carried a large pad, already mapped, with one page representing a square on the grid, and her job, as well as to participate in the digging, was to sketch the fossils as they were unearthed.

"Al uses a camera, too" she explained to Adam. "But it can't show exact distances, levels, and positions the way my illustrations can."

Adam's plan was to sketch several stages of the digging, as well, but he wanted to capture not the scientific data but the feel of it — the coulee, the sun, the distant mountains, and the people. Conversation drifted around him as he sat with his back against a boulder, his sketchbook on his bent knees, and got lost in the scene.

His first sketch showed kneeling, sitting, reclining, and stooping figures, some partially hidden by screens, most wearing gloves, some wearing knee pads, some with hat brims pulled down tightly to shade faces from thirty-five-degree temperatures, one Panama hat. Adam included the paraphernalia that was on hand — toilet paper, bags of plaster of Paris, two small barrels of water, and strips of burlap. Not to mentions bigger tools — shovels, picks, and grub hoes.

He wanted a "before" and "after" series entitled "Now and Then: What a Difference Seventy-Five Million Years Can Make." But the "before" and "after," he feared, would more likely apply before and after people found out he was a fake. He was a far cry from the "professional" Jamie had made him out to be.

"Hmm. You have quite a knack for that, son." Mr. Jamieson was looking down at Adam's work.

"Thanks. I'd like to do another one. Same place, but with the dinosaurs here building the nests."

"Sure. Interesting approach. You've got a pretty decent talent. It's funny Jamie's never mentioned you."

Adam felt the skin at the back of his neck begin to prickle. *Here it comes,* he thought. *He's going to ask questions I won't know how to answer.*

But Mr. Jamieson didn't. He tilted his head back and swept his arms around as though pulling Devil's Coulee into his chest. "This whole expanse of country was once a rich, lush garden. Just think of it. All those different breeds, each with its own specially adapted teeth, chomping and chomping away." He made chomping noises with his mouth.

Adam turned the page of his sketchbook and began a "before" drawing. For starters, he had decided to do a distant scene so that the dinosaurs were shrouded in mist and the details wouldn't have to be perfect.

CHAPTER 4

Insects, lizards, fish, frogs, crocodiles, turtles, and small mammals find their place, along with the dinosaurs, in the warm, moist habitat — feeding, breeding, sleeping, hunting and being hunted.

The monsoons have ended. It is wintertime, and the temperature is twenty-seven degrees Celsius. Creatures of every imaginable size, shape, and colour browse, hunt, and rest. Big animals, small animals, clumsy animals, graceful animals, horned, crested, crawling, burrowing, flying, and swimming animals.

Giant ostrich-like dinosaurs forage in large gaggles, running swiftly over the meadows, clawing small prey out of burrows and holes with their fore claws and then snatching them with quick strikes of their heads.

Flying Pterosaurs, *with ten-metre wingspans, swoop out of the sky to feed on small animals and decaying carcasses.* Crocodilians *crawl out of the swamps to bask in the sun. Small rat-like mammals scurry about in the undergrowth.*

The placid duckbills live together at the edge of swamps in extended family groups of a dozen or so, warning one another with trumpet-like calls when danger is near.

Hypacrosaurs *are one of these duckbills. They have large, flat snouts for cropping, and batteries of small grinding teeth cemented together allow them to eat needles and twigs of coniferous trees — forage other animals cannot digest. Their flashy facial crests culminate in bony ridges along their backs. The crests are not only useful echo chambers for their trombone-like courtship calls, but they are also exceptionally attractive to the opposite sex.*

Adam put down his pad and pencil, stood, stretched, and blinked.

"Listen, everybody!" Herbie was speaking loudly so the other group could hear. "If you come across anything that looks like elephant droppings, or doggy-doo, you know what to do. Call me."

"For sure, Herbie," Hans said. "We'll remember you're the manure man."

The plan was to remove individual eggs from some nests, but others they hoped to lift out whole. At each step of the way, as they exposed more and more of the eggs' surfaces by loosening the rock and dirt around them with hammers, picks, and a descending order of smaller and smaller tools and brushes, they painted them with glyptal, a polyvinyl acetate, to hold them together. They used long medicine droppers to drip the preservative into cracks and crevices. Eventually, when the fossil was almost free, they wrapped it in wet toilet paper and then put on a cast made of burlap strips soaked in plaster of Paris. They had to work fast once the plaster was mixed — it dried quickly in the sun. As they loosened the material around the eggs, they sifted the debris through a metal screen and picked out fragments of bone, shell, and other unidentifiable — to Adam at least — bits and pieces.

"It's ready. Come on, everybody. This is a moment to remember." Mr. Jamieson had set a camera on a tripod and was adjusting the focus. "Just hold everything for a couple of seconds while I get this thing set on time sequence."

Adam, along with the others, hurried to the nest and watched as careful hands cut through the pedestal supporting the egg.

"Beautiful piece of work," Mr. Jamieson said as he gingerly placed the fossil on a tripod made of pieces of sandstone. And it was — glistening white in the sunshine.

All was silent. The faint click of the camera shutter automatically opening and closing every few seconds seemed to be counting down through eons of time. This chunk of stone, which had last been exposed to the light of day too long ago for the human brain to comprehend, held an almost-hatched dinosaur baby. Adam shivered at the intensity of his own emotion.

He went back to his sketchpad. People found their voices and knelt beside the egg as if it were some kind of miracle, cheering, clapping, and watching as Mr. Jamieson labelled it.

Adam's pencil had taken on a life of its own, and he was simply the spectator, observing as simple strokes on paper became faces, bodies, shadows. He positioned the egg toward the lower left of the scene so that the slope of the hillside and the standing, kneeling, and squatting figures led the eye toward that focal point. Jamie's sturdy form seemed to anchor the group as she knelt with her hands on either side of her face, hiding her profile. Her braid swayed forward over one shoulder to hang like a dark tassel beside the dazzling egg. Adam was mesmerized by the images that were emerging on the page — the stark countryside, the people in prayer-like stances.

Suddenly, his pencil stopped moving and his attention jerked away from the paper. One figure stood apart, solemn and still. Bonnie seemed frozen, as if hypnotized. The experience must have been so overwhelming for her that she couldn't move or speak. Adam knew how she felt.

Hans glanced at his colleagues. "Yeah, you got the first one out, but ours will be better, won't it, guys?"

"Sure will," Lois said with a nod, reaching for her notebook. She had to be the biggest taker of notes Adam had ever seen.

"You bet," Sy said.

Mr. Jamieson moved to the other excavation site, squatted, and ran his hand around the contours of rock. "Looking good, but don't hurry it. It's doing fine right there in the matrix."

Adam kept his distance from the others as he walked back to camp. He needed to think. He had never before been with people like this. They were so focused, so involved in what they were doing, so connected. He wanted to be part of that connection, but he felt like an imposter. He wasn't a professional artist, he might not be able to draw a *Hypacrosaurus* to their satisfaction, and he and Jamie weren't old friends.

His conscience, together with his anxiety, was casting a cloud over what should have been one of the most thrilling experiences of his lifetime. By the time they were back in camp, he had firmly decided that, Jamie or no Jamie, he had to confess.

"Could I talk to you for a second?" he called to her.

"Sure." She stuck our her lower lip and blew up at her hair as she approached.

He stared at the ground. "Jamie, I feel like a dirty, lowdown, sneaky rat."

She laughed. "Well, like, maybe you are a dirty, lowdown, sneaky rat. You should know."

"Hey, give me a break, will you? I can't handle this any longer. I have to tell your dad the truth."

"Yeah, okay," she said nonchalantly with a toss of her head.

"You don't mind? I appreciate what you did getting me

in here, but enough is enough." Adam frowned and pushed his glasses firmly into place on the bridge of his nose.

"Sure, I understand. I'll tell him. It was my doing." She nudged a beetle that had landed on her arm, and it flew away in a flurry of black wings.

"I guess it'll be curtains for me, eh?" Adam kicked at a dandelion, sending seeds drifting slowly in the breathless air.

"Maybe not. I'll let you know what he says."

Adam tried to avoid the others, who were busy cleaning off their bits of bone and shell, comparing notes, labelling, writing in record books. He found a scraggly-looking child's toy broom and a bottle of window cleaner in a cupboard in Norm's place and he cleaned. He threw the doormat out on the ground and swept the floor. He cleaned all of the windows inside and out.

Other people moved around the camp area, but he avoided conversation with any of them. Sy wandered by, whistling a song Adam recognized — "Of All the Girls I've Loved Before." He waved and made his way between two tents toward his camper. Bonnie disappeared into her tent, carrying her kangaroos. Lois opened all the windows and ceiling vents in her van. Hans jumped on his mountain bike and pedalled off across the field. Meanwhile, Adam wiped out the sink with newspapers and cleaned the stovetop.

"Knock, knock. What are you doing? Want a shower? Everybody else has had theirs." Jamie was in the doorway. "And Dad says he wants to talk to you in about twenty minutes." She looked kind of nice in a windblown, outdoorsy way, with her hair out of its braid and held back with two Mickey Mouse barrettes.

"Yeah, I need one. Thanks." Adam turned back to the stove.

"Um, have I done something? You seem mad at me."
Jamie raised her hands, palms up, puzzled.

"No. It's not your fault. I feel lousy."

"So, like, we're not old friends." She shrugged. "But you sure can draw."

Sure, he could draw. He knew that, but could he draw well enough to satisfy true dinosaur lovers? It was like doing a portrait of somebody's golden-haired baby — trying to make it perfect enough to suit the parents.

"Catch you later." Jamie left.

"Yeah. Thanks." He grabbed a towel and rummaged in his pack for clean clothes.

Freshly showered, hair still damp, Adam went looking for Mr. Jamieson. He was wearing clean underwear and socks, the same denim shorts he had worn all day, though he had tried to shake the dust out of them, and a clean T-shirt. Knocking on the door of the Jamiesons' trailer, he gulped and squared his shoulders. He would take it like a man.

"Come." Mr. Jamieson was sitting on his heels and making notes while poking through a shoebox full of bones. He stood. "Come on in, son."

Adam's hopes rose. Mr. Jamieson had called him "son" as usual.

"Yes, well, now we might as well get straight to the point." Mr. Jamieson set his notebook on the table and placed the pen on top of it, precisely in the middle. "Jamie says she was mistaken about you being a professional artist. She just assumed that because your work impressed her so." He crossed his arms and leaned back against the table edge. "And she made up the old friend thing because she felt sorry for you. Can't blame her in a way. You did look pretty zonked. It took a heck of a lot of 'the right stuff,' as they say, to ride all the way from Calgary on a mission impossible."

Adam nodded. Should he try to explain his wish? More than a wish, his *need* to see the ancient nesting site of ancient animals? Mr. Jamieson would understand. He felt like that himself. So why explain?

"I like your drawings," Jamie's father continued.. "And I don't want to give you any false hope, but we might possibly, remember, I said might *possibly*, be able to use something. We're always on the lookout for designs for T-shirts, and we'll be needing a poster of the *Hypacrosaurus* and the nests for tourist promotion. Stick around for a couple of days and give it a try, if you like. Just remember one thing — you'll be doing it on spec."

"Pardon? I can stay? You mean it?" Adam's hand shot out for a shake, and he grinned and nodded several times. "I'll draw anything. I'm probably not good enough for posters, but I'd sure like to try. Thanks a lot! Thanks a whole lot, Mr. Jamieson!"

Mr. Jamieson smiled. "Please, son, call me Al."

Adam felt like an honest man again as he strolled back to Norm's place. Drawings for T-Shirts? A *Hypacrosaurus* for posters? Maybe? Just maybe! The thrill was mingled with anxiety. He probably couldn't live up to Mr. Jamieson's — Al's — expectations. His sketchpads were full of awesome-looking predators, swift scavengers, and powerful airborne vertebrates, but he had never paid much attention to duckbills, so he probably wouldn't get it right. But at least he could stay and try.

CHAPTER 5

Near the edge of the forests, on one of the deltas, a small herd of Hypacrosaurs *graze. The babies have grown into six-metre-long, 300-kilogram one-year-olds. The five-year-olds, on the verge of adulthood, are up to ten metres long and weigh two to three tonnes.*

A six-year-old female lifts her head, sniffs the air, and gives a low snort. Immediately, all heads are up. A wave of restlessness ripples through the group. Distant sounds — thumping hooves and bleating calls — fill the air. Time to go!

The small herd moves to join the running mob — thousands of them, all heading for the nesting site 160 kilometres away.

The young female loses track of her three surviving offspring, hatched a year ago, but they are somewhere in the middle of the adults, safe from attack. She will soon have new babies to care for. She lopes along on her powerful hind legs, her long, flattened tail held out behind her for balance. Her head bobs forward and back as she runs.

It will take several days to reach the mud flats where the nests are always built. The countryside reverberates with the mating calls of many different animals as they bleat, snort, and trumpet, blowing through their nose holes. The journey is fraught with danger. Meat eaters are always on the prowl.

Adam's sketch showed one animal standing in a swamp, wide-eyed, listening. Her muscular back legs easily supported her weight, her neck was arched, her head was up, her small forearms were raised near her chest. Her facial crest and her wide-lipped mouth reminded Adam, strangely, of a girl he had once tried to paint. She had worn a red sailor hat with the brim pinned back, and her face had held the same look of artlessness.

The supper gong sounded, and Adam reluctantly put his pad away. The dinosaur's presence seemed so strong that he could hear her breathing and smell her sweat. He had to give her a name. She had enough impressive names now to satisfy even the most classification-conscious scientist. She was of the order *Ornithischia*, suborder *Ornithopoda*, and her family name was *Hadrosauridae*. So she sure didn't need another one of those. He decided to call her Hya.

Supper was served in the cookhouse at one long table with benches along both sides. An extra-large stove was at one end of the trailer, while an extra-large refrigerator stood against the wall at right angles to it. The power supply was provided by a portable electric generator.

Adam filled his plate from the pots on the stove and sat beside Bonnie. She was as animated now as she had been immobilized earlier. "Hi, sweetie. Doesn't that boggle the mind, digging up that old egg?"

"You bet," Adam said. "Is the University of Alberta pretty good for paleontology? I assume that's your major?"

Bonnie nodded emphatically. "You got it right on both counts, sweetie. We have top-notch people. Nothing but the best."

"What year are you in?"

"Going into fourth."

"Good stew," Adam said as Sy edged in on the other side of him, still wearing his Panama hat.

"You betcha," Sy said. "Sure smells good. One thing you can count on around here is good eats. You don't get paid, but you sure get fed." He settled in and started to stuff his face.

A little later the music and laughter grew louder as Adam strolled toward the campfire. He sat on the ground at the end of a bench where Jamie was seated. Slim was in good form. He had one foot resting on an overturned pail, and the studs on his jeans and the wide silver buckle on his belt reflected the firelight. His face was half hidden under his hat brim — the perfect picture of a cowboy singing beside the campfire. "To be free again, just to be again where the bloom is on the sage," he warbled.

The music stopped, and Slim acknowledged the applause with a tip of his hat.

Jamie stood. "Want to go for a walk?"

Adam was beside her in an instant. "Sure."

As they moved out of the circle of firelight, Jamie waved to her father, then pointed at Adam and off into the distance. He nodded and waved back.

"Would you call this a cow path?" Adam asked as Jamie led the way along a meandering trail that wound through the pasture.

"I guess. Since there are cows." She indicated a herd of twenty animals silhouetted against the moonlit grass. "Have you ever milked one?"

"No. And I can't say I've ever wanted to. Have you?"

"Sure. Want to try? It's not hard."

Surely, she was joking. Or was she? Could refusing to milk a cow be called stodgy? "You mean, we just walk up to a strange cow, say, 'So, bossy,' and milk it? Just like that?"

"Sure. Why not? Just enough to get the hang of it. I don't mean really milk it."

"I think I can live without that experience," Adam said.

Stodgy or not, the idea of milking somebody else's cow, even if he had known how to do it, wasn't his type of adventure. "Hey, there's Sy. He's looking around that oil well. What can he possibly find so interesting about that? They're all the same, bobbing away night and day, up and down, up and down." Adam raised and lowered his hand as he spoke. "They remind me of a mechanical woodpecker I used to have when I was a kid."

"Yeah, but he thinks each one has a different personality," Jamie said. "Like pets or something."

Adam watched as Sy stopped walking and tilted his head back to look at the sky.

"Does he ever take that hat off?" Adam asked.

"I've never seen him without it," Jamie said. "Even when he takes a shower he sets it on the corner post and comes out wearing it."

"Really? I guess it's his security blanket. What's yours?"

Jamie shrugged. "I don't know. I guess it would be my dinosaur teeth. They make me feel connected somehow."

"Dinosaur teeth? You're kidding?" He studied her. "You're not kidding."

"No, I'm not kidding. I've been collecting for as long as I can remember, and they tell me things. Each one has its own story. How about you?"

"My security blanket? Drawing. I can't imagine life without it." Now that they were away from the smell of the campfire, Adam sniffed appreciatively at the delicate mix of scents in the air. He wished he could identify them all. There was wild rose, and a pungent mushroomy smell, as well as grass and something that reminded him of turkey stuffing — sage, that was it.

They reached an eroded area about the size of a room

at the foot of a low hill. Jamie bent over and walked around slowly, picking up bits of stone and bone, placing some back in exactly the same position in which she had found them and putting others in a plastic bag she had pulled from her pocket.

"Hey, it is okay to do this, right?" Adam asked.

"Of course." Her reply was abrupt.

"Well, I, uh …" Adam felt embarrassed, as though he had asked his art instructor if it was all right to draw. "No. I mean, you wouldn't be doing it if it wasn't. You know a million times more about all this than I do. But —"

"It's already been combed for any useful stuff that's on top," she said. "But just a couple of days ago I found a little jawbone, only about this big." She spread her thumb and forefinger about seven centimetres. "It's perfect — from a baby *Maiasaurus*. I'm going to get a Certified Fossil Finder Certificate for it."

Adam chuckled.

"What?" Jamie asked.

"Oh, nothing. I shouldn't say it. What if Herbie gets one?"

Jamie looked puzzled, then giggled. "That's not nice. *Thertified Fothil Finder Thertificate.*"

"I know," Adam said. "It's a cheap shot. Herbie's a nice guy, and I sure wouldn't mind having his smarts."

Jamie picked up a small object and turned it over. "Teeth are a dime a dozen. Dinosaurs could lose teeth and grow new ones for as long as they lived." She put the object in the bag.

"Really? I wonder what the tooth fairy would leave a dinosaur?"

"Maybe a big juicy palm leaf?"

"Yeah. I'm glad I didn't have to try to slip a palm leaf under a dinosaur's pillow." Adam pantomimed doing just that while Jamie laughed and applauded.

Hey! He had made her laugh. Maybe there was some hope for him, after all.

A glimmer of golden light in an eroded patch just below the top of the hill attracted Adam's attention. "What's this?"

"Amber," she said excitedly. "A nice one. Maybe you can keep it, as long as there's not an insect or seeds in it."

Adam was excited, too. The amber was about the size of a robin's egg, but he couldn't pull it loose from where it was embedded in hard dirt.

"Here." Jamie pulled a pocketknife from her belt.

"You must have been a Girl Scout. Be prepared — that's got to be your motto." Adam opened the knife and leaned close to the bank as he worked.

Jamie watched. "Careful. Always cut or pick away from a fossil, because sometimes shock waves can damage them."

"Thanks." He leaned closer.

"Nice one," Jamie said as Adam pulled the amber free and held it in his hand. She rolled it around in his palm with her forefinger. "Hold it up, see if it looks clear. There might be something in it."

"Yeah, shades of *Jurassic Park.* Maybe there's a mosquito in there with a drop of dinosaur blood in its gut. DNA just waiting for a chance to do its stuff, like in the movie."

The amber was clear except for one small area that still had some hard mud sticking to it.

"That'll come off with a little acid," Jamie said. "Herbie's rigged up an acid bath."

When they returned to camp, the party was winding down. Sy was back, people were sitting in pairs or small groups talking quietly, and the fire was dying. Slim had put his ukulele away.

Jamie showed the amber to her father. "Can Adam keep it?"

"Probably," Al said. "I'll have a better look tomorrow under the microscope, but keep it for now." He smiled at Jamie's obvious pleasure in handing the amber back to Adam.

"I found me a decent-sized piece of amber a couple of years ago in an old coal mine," Sy said.

Slim stood, yawned, and stretched. "I'm gonna hit the sack." He picked up his ukulele case, Bonnie picked up her kangaroos, and the group dispersed.

Adam decided to take a chance and ask somebody's opinion of his sketch of Hya. Jamie was the easiest one, so he asked her.

"Yeah, it looks good," she said as she shone a flashlight on the page. "I think the front legs should be a little shorter, and maybe the ridge on the back should be higher, but I like the face. Show it to some of the others. Herbie would know for sure, and my dad."

Adam was feeling good as he climbed back into the camper. He didn't have to keep up the "old friend" pretense, everyone seemed to accept him, Jamie thought he could be a decent duckbill artist, and he might actually be making some headway in the anti-stodginess department.

He found an egg cup and placed the amber in it. It *was* pretty in the candlelight. What a great gift to take back to his mother. He set the egg cup on the windowsill and thought about his real reason for being here. Hya. Maybe on her hazardous journey she had loped right past the very tree the amber had come from.

Now that the Hypacrosaurs *are out in the open, they are more vulnerable to attack. Such large herds attract several kinds of predators, each adapted to a particular method of killing.*

Hya smells a killer, hears a loud snort, careens, the herd swerves. A stalking Albertosaurus *has found and is chasing down an unwary old male. He screeches. The older females bellow warnings and swoosh their tails from side to side.*

The Albertosaurus *lunges at the head and neck of the old bull. He stumbles. Powerful jaws crush through his neck in one crunch. Although the* Albertosaurus *is no larger than its victim, its backward-slanting, sharp, serrated teeth soon rip the other animal to shreds. There is the smell of blood in the air.*

Another adult, a cow with a limp, falls prey to a pack of running Dromeosaurs. *These speedy, agile, large-brained predators kill in a different way. Each has a sickle-shaped claw on both hind feet, which they hold up while they run. The* Hypacrosaurus *screams in agony as the horrible claws slash through her skin and flesh again and again. The hunters attack and retreat, attack and retreat. She staggers. She falls. The herd runs on.*

Hya snorts with fear, runs as close in to the others as possible, watching to see that the juveniles stay in the middle of the herd.

The next morning the sun was well up from the horizon at 7:00 a.m. The hot, dry wind rippled the short grass and whipped the dust around the eroded areas. The people, carrying packs on their backs and canvas bags in their hands, laughed and bantered on the hike to the dig.

Jamie and Bonnie were a few steps ahead of Adam. Bonnie suddenly raised her head, lost her footing on some caliche nodules, and grabbed at Jamie's arm for support as the weight of her pack pulled her off balance.

Adam caught the backpack and lifted it with one hand, helping Bonnie regain her balance, while with the other hand he reached for Jamie to keep her from falling. Her other hand was holding her own backpack in an awkward position, and she had her head tilted back to keep her sunglasses from slipping off. He snatched the glasses, still holding her hand, then jerked his hand away from hers as the glasses slipped from his fingers. Adam tried unsuccessfully to catch them before they landed on the ground and almost lost his own footing as he scrambled around on the gravelly path. Finally, he held them up. They were covered with dust.

He felt itchy all over and he was gasping. What a fool he was making of himself! "Sorry," he blurted. "Trying to do too many things at once."

"No sweat. You saved us both from a fall." Jamie turned her back to him. "Would you adjust my shoulder straps?"

Adam took longer than was necessary fiddling with the straps so that by the time she turned to face him again he had regained his composure. "How's that?" He gave her shoulder a little pat.

"That is just absolutely, perfectly, wonderfully fine," she said, tilting her chin and smiling at him in a teasing way.

Adam tried to think of a clever response, but all he could come up with was "Good." He wanted very badly at that moment to sound worldly and witty — to change the opinion she must have of him. He was not only stodgy, but now he had just proved himself a clumsy dolt. Worldly and witty? What a laugh! He was about as worldly as a cactus and as witty as a fossil. Until Grade Five Adam had considered himself, if not popular, at least attractive to some members of the opposite sex, but then all of the girls had seemed to grow centimetres a day while he had maintained a steady stature on the short side. He had avoided standing beside girls, sitting beside girls, walking near girls, and most of all, talking to girls. He had been certain he had looked like an open-mouthed toad to them, with his head back and his Adam's apple bobbing when he peered up into their faces.

So he had thrown himself into his dinosaur world with increased intensity. His drawing had provided an escape, a solace, and a warm glow of satisfaction when he managed to produce a portrait of an extinct animal that seemed alive enough to walk off the page.

Finally, he'd had a growth spurt when he was fifteen, but by then he had become so accustomed to considering himself a zero with women that he hadn't given the matter much serious consideration. Until now. Now he wished he had paid attention when he had heard other guys talk about girls. Not that he cared about anything romantic with Jamie — she was too off-the-wall for him, and besides she definitely wasn't his idea of feminine.

Adam took a deep breath and resolved to change things. He would start practising tai chi again to improve his balance and coordination, and he would try to be more sharp-witted with words.

"Poaching? Really?" Hans's voice interrupted Adam's thoughts. They had reached the dig, and people were squatting and pulling tools from their packs.

Al nodded. "Yeah. Nasty business. I'm sure this site's safe enough, but there have been a few instances near here."

Adam stopped dead in his tracks. "Are you serious? Do people really steal fossils?"

"You bet they do," Al said. "Fossils of any kind are the new collecting craze. A good one can be worth tens of thousands of dollars on the international black market."

"Yeah, man, we're talking mega-bucks," Mike said, and headed off to his micro site.

"And a whole egg would be a real humdinger," Sy said. He adjusted his Panama hat to shade his forehead from the sun. "The sucker could be worth, oh, say up to twenty thou."

CHAPTER 6

Adam tried to sketch, but nothing seemed to work. The wind carried dust and pollen, making his eyes itch and his face burn. He used insect repellent and then couldn't decide which he hated more — the feel and smell of the repellent or the whine and sting of the bugs. His dinosaurs looked like long-tailed rhinoceroses with short front legs, and the vine-covered trees he drew belonged on a kids' backyard obstacle course.

Adam placed his pad on a flat rock and climbed the hill to see how Mike was doing. Mike was more exposed to wind and dust than the others, and he was wearing a Tilley hat hung with a curtain of mosquito netting. His knees were protected with pads, and he had taken off one of his leather gloves and was examining something with a small magnifying glass attached to a cord. A paperback novel was tucked into a crevice in the closest hoodoo.

Adam read the book's title. "*Skinwalkers*. So you're a Tony Hillerman fan."

"Yes, sir," Mike said. "I find it's the best escape therapy there is. The way Hillerman describes the desert landscape is awesome, man."

"Yeah?" Adam said. "I've never read anything of his. He throws in a little witchcraft, doesn't he?"

"He does so. Myth and legend and religious practices of the Navajo."

Adam hunkered down beside him. "What have you got there?"

"Could be a skin impression. What do you think?" Mike handed the lens to Adam.

Adam peered at the thing Mike was holding. He couldn't see anything except a piece of shale. "Um … I don't know what skin is supposed to look like."

"There, see?" Mike traced an outline of faint ridges with his finger.

"Oh, yeah …" Adam pretended enlightenment, which he didn't feel, and handed the glass back. "Tell me about this micro site business. I'm a real airhead about that sort of thing."

Mike stretched one leg and bent the other knee. "It's a certain way of looking at the world. Small is beautiful. There's a whole universe to explore in a fishbone, or a piece of turtle shell. You look for the smallest clues. You don't need a five-tonne skeleton to tell you about prehistory. Flies, seeds, snails — it's all there. 'To see the world in a grain of sand,' as William Blake put it. A frog skeleton is an incredible work of nature, and the fossilized impression of a damsel fly? Man, talk about an adrenaline rush!"

"I'm impressed. I can see why you like mystery novels — small clues add up. I'd like to try sketching some of your seeds, frogs, and bugs sometime, if you could fill me in a bit."

"Sure thing, guy." Mike adjusted his knee pads and went back to work.

Everybody seemed to grow tired and irritable as the morning wore on, probably the inevitable letdown after the thrill of yesterday's success.

People quibbled over small things. "Isn't that my dental pick?" Bonnie asked sharply.

"*Sorr-ee*. How could I be so careless?" Lois replied.

"Aren't you forgetting something, young fella?" Sy demanded.

"No, what am I forgetting?" Hans asked, chin jutting out.

"Chip away from the fossil," Sy said archly. "Away from it. Not toward it. The shock waves can cause —"

"I know that," Hans interrupted impatiently. "What do you think I'm doing? Jousting?"

By noon even Al had given up trying to be cheerful. The sun broiled the body, and the wind sucked it dry. Dust had seeped into every crack and crevice at Devil's Coulee.

Adam had grit in his ears, eyes, nose, armpits, and crotch. He seemed to be breathing grit, feeling grit, tasting grit, and stepping on grit inside his shoes.

"We're quitting early," Al finally said. "Let's work another half-hour and then we'll head to the reservoir for a swim."

"A swim?" Herbie cried. "A real swim? In real water? The whole body immersed in it. Right on! God, paradise calls."

"Al, you're the greatest!" Lois said.

"That would be wonderful!" Denise seconded.

"A swim." Jamie stood and started doing breaststroke motions in the air. "The Devonian Sea is calling us back to our primal beginnings. Can we skinny-dip, Dad?" She laughed at her father's mock scowl and changed to the side stroke.

An hour later they were back in camp, and soon people appeared out of tents and trailers carrying towels.

Hans didn't want to go — he was going to have a long shower, since not many people would be needing the water, and then do some cycling to keep in shape for the B.C. Championship mountain bike races coming up at Whistler Mountain in September.

Sy was standing beside his camper.

"We've got room," Herbie called. "Come with us."

"No," Sy said. "Never was much of a swimmer. Thanks, anyway. I'll take me a little walk. I get a charge out of looking at the oil wells. See if those jokers have been doing a good job."

"Aren't you coming, Bonnie?" Jamie asked as she crawled into the back seat of her father's Jeep.

Bonnie shook her head. She had changed her clothes and was wearing a halter top and bikini-style shorts, and was carrying a tin pail with a length of twine knotted through holes punched in the sides. "No thanks, sweetie. Swimming isn't my thing. I'd rather go saskatoon picking. The cook said he'd make pies if I get enough for four pies." She waved the empty pail and wandered away.

"You can ride with me, Adam," Herbie said. "Just give me a hand taking these out first, will you?" He opened the front hood of his Volkswagen.

There were two plastic trays with liquid in them covering an assortment of fossilized clams, snails, teeth, claws, and small bones. "This is an acid bath — not very strong, just vinegar — but it dissolves the limestone. I rigged it up here so I can close the hood and keep it out of harm's way." Herbie poked several of the fossils, turning them over.

Adam helped lift the trays and hold them steady. They set them inside Herbie's tent. The tent flaps were hooked back, and Herbie left them that way. "Air the place out," he said.

The reservoir was ten kilometres away. Slim was settling himself in the shade of a tree while Al, Jamie, Mike, and Denise were already in the water when Herbie, Lois, and Adam chugged up in the Beetle.

Jamie stood poised in knee-deep water, then let herself fall backward with a splash. "It's heavenly," she called, and began to propel herself around on her back, using her hands like little paddles above her head.

It *was* heavenly. The air was full of the smell of water and trees and felt soft and moist on hot, dry skin. Adam stepped out of his shorts and dived in. The first shock of cold took his breath away, but within seconds he thought he knew exactly what Jamie meant when she talked about hearing the call of the ancient sea where life began. He let his muscles relax, moved his arms and legs only enough to keep afloat, and absorbed the sensation. He knew this was one of those moments he would remember — the intense pleasure of the sudden change from an unbearably hot and sticky body to a sensually cool and stimulated one.

Adam thought about Mike and his reverence for small things and tried to imagine the ancient life forms, the very one-celled creatures that had led to his own existence, floating around as he was now. Mentally, he drew a series of pictures. The first one was of blue-green algae — that was all there was during the Precambrian period and that was where the one-celled guys had gotten their start. Then had come marine invertebrates. He would represent them by a trilobite. The first fish were followed, eons later, by the first traces of land life — a monster scorpion for that one. What would be the most appropriate representation for the Devonian period? Amphibians had started to appear then, and the first land snails and primitive land plants. The sea was full of anemones, grasses, corals, fan-shaped clams, and a type of squid that looked like upside-down carrots. And that huge fish — a dunk-something.

Jamie was pulling herself out of the water and onto a

raft, and Adam remembered his witty conversation promise to himself.

"Hey, Jamie." He swam toward the raft in his most masterful stroke, the butterfly. "What's the name of that dunka-whatever-it-was that lived in the Devonian Sea? The big guy?"

Jamie was holding her head sideways and pounding her lowered ear with the palm of her hand.

"Pardon?" She stopped pounding but kept her hand against her ear. Her wet hair was plastered to her shoulders, and her eyelashes sparkled with water drops in the amber-tinged light of the sun.

"Water in your ear?" Adam asked as he climbed out and sat beside her, letting his legs dangle in the water. Now there was a clever thing to say!

"How did you guess?" Jamie asked, laughing. She gave her ear one last thump and raised her head. "You must be some kind of genius to figure that one out."

Jamie had that teasing look on her face again, and Adam's mind searched for a quick and witty retort. "Hey, my powers of deduction are extremely sharp." He winked. "Young woman seen swimming in water. Young woman climbs out, sits on raft. Young woman hits ear with palm of hand. We can only surmise water in ear of young woman."

Not exactly witty, he decided, but better than nothing.

"Or maybe young woman likes ear-pounding sensation," Jamie suggested. "Different strokes for different folks." She moved closer to Adam, and her arm brushed against him. "Could you repeat the question?"

"The question?" Adam's brain had stopped functioning at the feel of her skin. What was this all about? It must be something like earthquake aftershock, he told himself. Not the real thing, but the result of what had gone on before. This was the aftermath of the pleasure of the swim. "The question? Oh, yeah, the question. What's the name of that dunk-what's-his-face that lived in the Devonian Sea? The biggest guy?" Adam stirred the water with his feet.

"That was *Dunkleosteus*, ten metres long, big as dinosaurs." Jamie stretched her arms and smacked her palms together in a gobbling motion. "I'm *Dunkleosteus*, and I'm going to eat you up," she said in a growly voice. Her feet splashed up and down in little kicks.

"Hey, don't eat me. Eat Middle Billy Goat Gruff. She's much tastier than I," Adam said, grabbing Jamie's arm and examining it as though looking for a tender spot in which to sink his teeth. "Pass the salt."

Jamie laughed, pulled her arm away, and hugged herself.

Adam no longer felt like a dolt. In fact, he was beginning to relax and enjoy this silliness. It didn't seem so hard, but then this was only Jamie. With a girl he really wanted to impress it would probably be a lot harder. Still, this wasn't bad. Not bad at all for a beginner at sparkling conversation.

They were silent for several minutes, lulled by the hypnotic motion of the raft, the rhythmic sound of water lapping against the buoy, and the distant images of trees and people absorbed in a slow and wavering dance in the shimmering heat. Adam drifted into a trancelike state where there was no need for words and yet a strange kind of communication was happening.

Lois climbed onto the raft and told them about the rose mallow she and Denise had found at lunchtime, and the baby pronghorn they had seen bouncing along as if it had invented the world.

Adam tried to think of a way to ride home in the Jeep with Jamie, but he didn't see how he could switch without hurting Herbie's feelings. The Volkswagen was old, rusty, and bruised, but it seemed to be Herbie's pride and joy, so Adam said, "Good old reliable Beetle," and patted the roof as he crawled in.

"We'll put the acid baths back after supper when it's cooler," Herbie said when they arrived back at camp.

CHAPTER 7

Adam, refreshed and energized by the swim, sat outside and thought about this different world he was now inhabiting — where small was as awesome as big, where lilies and birdsongs and a baby pronghorn were more thrilling than skiing and rock groups and Olympic Games. The thought sobered him. Where had he missed out? He envied Lois and Denise their sense of awe and wonder at the natural world. He had been a hermit living in his own little shell, thinking the only things that could be thrilling were extinct animals. He would try to change that.

One more thing to change! My God, next thing he knew he would decide to become a Buddhist, grow a beard, and renounce worldly wealth!

Thinking of Buddhism reminded him of tai chi. He had mastered the basics, hoping to move on to karate, but after watching several demonstrations he had come to the conclusion that neither his body nor his personality were karate-friendly. His body was too chunky and his personality was too — what was the word? Cautious? Tentative? Reclusive? Stodgy!

"Real guys" didn't do tai chi in his circle of friends, so he made light of his lessons, claiming they were just preparation for one of the more aggressive martial arts.

The supper gong sounded.

The sun was close to the horizon, and Adam was standing on a patch of grass doing some stretching and balancing without his shirt on when Herbie asked, "Will you give me a hand to put these back, Adam?"

"Sure will." Adam did some elbow bends as he headed across to Herbie's tent.

"Huh? That's funny." Herbie was kneeling over one of the acid trays and sounded puzzled. "A jaw seems to be missing. With virgin teeth."

Jaw? Virgin? Herbie must be talking about something to do with fossils, but virgin?

"Um … jaw?" Adam asked. "Missing?"

"Yeah. There was a jaw in here from a baby. Just hatched. Complete set of teeth in it — never been used to chew. And it's gone." He stared at the tray again, nudged some of the contents aside, looked all around.

"Gone?" Adam was standing at the open tent flap and poked his head inside.

Herbie bent down to lift one side of a tray, and Adam crouched to pick up the other.

"A jaw, you say?" Adam was beginning to feel like a ventriloquist's dummy. They carried the soaking fossils to the car.

Herbie nodded absentmindedly. "Yeah. But what the heck. I guess it'll turn up. Maybe Jamie took it out. Or Al."

They put the other tray in the car, and Herbie started to close the hood, hesitated, then opened it again.

"What?" Adam asked. "Something else?"

"I'm not sure." Herbie shook his head. "Probably not. I think I'm losing it. Getting paranoid. I'll get out my list and check it later."

Adam went back into the camper for his shirt. Something

was amiss. He looked around. The egg cup was in a different position, and it was empty.

Jamie appeared at the door. "What's up, Doc?"

"It's gone." Adam turned the egg cup upside down.

"What's gone?"

"The amber. I put it in here last night."

"Your amber? Gone?"

"That's what I said. See, gone." He shook the cup impatiently. "Empty, vacant, without contents."

"Huh? Your amber really is gone? Unless. Did you put it somewhere else?"

There she goes again, he thought, *making me feel like a dumb little kid.*

"Jamie, for God's sake, give me credit for a gram or two of grey matter, will you? If I say it's gone, it's gone! Here, you see if you can find it in there." He thrust the cup angrily toward her.

"Okay, okay, I'm sorry. Just cool it," she said soothingly, pushing his hand away. "I didn't mean it that way. But it seems impossible. What could have happened to it?"

"What do you think? Somebody wanted it, obviously." He turned and set the cup on the table with a bang.

"No," Jamie said, waving her hands in front of her face, palms out. "Nobody would just take it."

Adam wheeled to face her. "You mean *steal* it, don't you?"

"Adam." Jamie stepped into the camper. "If it really is stolen, then we're not going to get very far arguing like this. Let's put our heads together and think about it."

"You're right." Adam's anger subsided, and as it did, he remembered something else. "Have you talked to Herbie?"

She shook her head. "Why?"

"He said there might be something missing from the

acid bath. A little dinosaur jaw."

"Oh, no!" Jamie looked alarmed. "The one I found? That I'm getting a certificate for?"

"I guess. Was there more than one?"

"Not that I know of." She stared past Adam's shoulder with her teeth clamped shut and her forehead furrowed. "What's going on? Aw, it has to be some kind of mistake." She squared her shoulders. "I'm going to talk to Herbie right now."

Adam watched Jamie cross the road, heard her call Herbie's name, and when there was no response, she hurried away.

Adam stood in the doorway and looked around. Sy was crouched down, fiddling with something under his camper. Hans was sitting on his haunches beside his bicycle. The frame was upside down, the rest of it was scattered about on the ground in bits and pieces, and he was working with a small tool. Bonnie was reclining on a canvas lounge chair with a book on her lap and a pencil in her hand.

On an impulse Adam decided to have a little chat with his neighbours. Somebody must have taken his amber. Maybe one of them? Maybe somebody had just borrowed it to check it out for seeds or other organic matter. If so, seeing him should remind the borrower to mention the fact.

"Bicycle problems?" Adam asked, strolling toward Hans.

Hans nodded. "Tube juncture could be cracked. See that wrinkled paint?" He rubbed his grease-covered hand gently along a spot on the frame.

"Oh, yeah, right," Adam said. "Could be." He had always thought a bicycle was just a two-wheeled thing you rode. It might need its tires pumped up once in a while, but it had never occurred to him that it could need the kind of loving attention Hans was giving his.

"Did you have a good ride this afternoon?" Adam asked.

Hans kept on working. "Yep. Those steep hills are a great workout."

"Are there trails, or do you just take your chances?"

"There are trails of sorts, but nothing to write home about. Come on, baby, don't seize up on me." Hans bit his lower lip and pushed on the wrench a little harder.

"So you didn't look for fossils or amber or anything then?" Adam watched Hans's face for any reaction, but he seemed to be totally involved in his baby's seized-up bolt.

"Would you hand me the WD-40?" he asked.

Adam searched around for the tin. Spread out on the ground were sprockets, a tire pump, pedals, greasy rags, and more bits and pieces of bicycle than Adam knew existed, but he couldn't see a tin of WD-40. "I don't see it. Could it be in the bag?" A large canvas bag was lying near the tent.

"No, no," Hans said. "Nothing in there but dirty laundry. Um, maybe under that rag." He pointed.

It was under a greasy rag, and Hans grunted his thanks when Adam handed him the can with a little red plastic tube attached.

Bonnie was still on her lounge chair, pencil poised, staring into the distance. "Hi, sweetie. What's a six-letter word for *ludicrous*?" She waved a crossword puzzle book as Adam approached.

"Um, any clues?" Adam asked. "What letters have you got?"

"None so far." A twig snapped, and she shuddered. "What was that?"

"Just the heat, or maybe a deer," Adam said. "Absurd."

"Yeah, I know, sweetie. I get jumpy sometimes."

"No, I mean the crossword. *Absurd* is a six-letter word for *ludicrous*."

"*Ri-i-ight!*" Bonnie smacked her forehead with the palm of her hand. "Thanks." She started to pencil in the letters.

Sy was sitting on a camp stool cleaning something with rubbing alcohol. "Greetings," he said to Adam.

"Yeah, right on," Adam said. "What have you got there?"

"Chert. Indians used it for arrowheads. Isn't that a dandy?" He held it up and turned it for Adam to admire.

"Dandy. Did you find it this afternoon?"

Sy shook his head. "Didn't go out. It was so consarned hot I just lazed around, had me forty winks and a boo at the latest newspaper I could find." He nodded toward the cookhouse where a box of recyclable newspapers and magazines was kept. "I'll take a walk later when it cools off."

"Um … nobody else around this afternoon to keep you company, I guess?" Adam ventured.

"No. Bonnie wandered by a few times to empty her pail. She's a whirlwind of a berry picker, that girl." Sy poked a finger up under his Panama hat to scratch his head. "Here comes the whiz kid."

Jamie was walking along the road.

"See you later." Adam went to meet her.

The whiz kid wasn't feeling very whizzy. In fact, she seemed pretty agitated as they settled themselves on the ground in the shade of Norm's camper.

"It's impossible, but I guess it's true," she said, and started yanking blades of grass. "My dad's really upset. He's never had anything like this happen before. Never. All the years he's worked on digs. He doesn't know what to do."

"Stuff really is missing then?"

She nodded and sighed. "Yeah. The jaw, some of the pieces Mike found at the micro site. My teeth. Plus your amber. How can this be happening?" Her voice quavered.

"That's rotten luck, Jamie. I'm really sorry about your teeth and the jaw. Were they in the Prowler?"

She shook her head. "I left them in a box in the fossil hut. What a bummer. Don't mention it to anybody. Dad wants to keep it quiet for now. It will really wreck morale if people find out that they're working their buns off without getting paid and a low-life is stealing stuff." She clenched her hands together. "The teeth are bad enough. I've spent hours collecting them. But the jaw — I'll probably never find another one."

"I'm sorry, Jamie. It's a bad scene."

"I simply can't imagine how anybody could get in through the fence, go into the fossil hut, Herbie's tent, your camper, grab stuff, and get out again without somebody seeing him." She picked a stalk of wheat grass and started jabbing it into the eyelets of her hiking boots.

"Hey, but isn't it possible it could be an inside job?" Adam suggested.

Jamie's head jerked up and she stared at him. "What?"

"An inside job. What if it's an inside job?"

She shook her head. "No." There was a trace of scorn in her voice. "You've met them all. Which one would you say could be a thief? Come on. Which one of the people on this dig could pull such a dirty trick?"

Adam was a little hurt by her immediate dismissal of his suggestion, so he had to convince her that it wasn't totally dumb. "Yeah, I'm sure you're right, but consider the possibility. Remote though it may seem, stranger things have happened."

Jamie lowered her head and looked thoughtful. "I guess. I don't believe it for a minute, but …"

"Well, for starters, somebody on the inside could get away with it a lot easier. And when it comes to money, you'd be surprised. You wouldn't believe the people who shoplift at the drugstore where I work — one woman wearing a mink coat and enough diamonds to start a jewellery store took a bottle of shampoo. Would you believe it? Shampoo — worth a dollar eighty-nine. Slipped it in her pocket. Nice lady. Always had a kind word. Her husband's a doctor. So there you go, Jamie. You just never know. And even if it isn't somebody on the inside, it's not going to hurt to think about the possibility."

"Okay, okay. Enough already. I'll admit it's possible." She frowned and studied the wheat grass intently, turning it around as though it might tell her something. "Okay, just for the sake of argument, we'll say it's an inside job," she said finally. "Then we have to catch him."

"What?"

Jamie leaned toward him and enunciated the words slowly. "We have to catch him."

"Just like that."

"Just like that. And before everybody finds out what's going on."

"And how, my dear private eye, do you suggest we go about this catching business?"

She stood and stretched. "We'll think of a way. Sleep on it and try to come up with a plan."

"Okay, Lieutenant, sir!" He jumped up and saluted. "Your wish is my command. I'll sleep on it, but don't expect miracles from this hombre."

"It doesn't have to be a miracle, just a plan. We'll do a bit of snooping around."

Adam was suspicious. "Snooping around where?"

"Tents, packs, you know, places where the stuff could be stashed."

"Jamie! You can't do that. You can't search through people's belongings without their permission."

"No, no, no, no. I don't exactly mean *search*. I just mean, uh, a bit of poking around. You know?"

So what would be her definition of poking around? Adam decided not to ask.

The idea of making a plan with Jamie — whispered conferences, shared secrets, conversations about confidential information — sounded like fun in a way. Then he remembered that he was the newcomer. What if people suspected him? His mind raced as he tried to think of anything he had done or said that might have given them that idea.

And what plans would Jamie come up with? She hadn't hesitated to stretch the truth about him, she had thought there was nothing wrong with milking other people's cows in the middle of the night, and she had said "poking around" would be okay.

Adam hadn't noticed the growing darkness, but now the stars were beginning to appear and the evening had that stillness about it when wild creatures got ready to sleep or hunt. The vehicles, tents, and trailers were like a movie set — too perfect to be real in the soft bluish light.

He couldn't keep his mind focused on a few missing bones and a piece of amber in that hushed and fragrant world. The smells of ripening berries, wild roses, creeping juniper, and wild parsley seemed secretive and sweet, as though they were there only for him.

CHAPTER 8

Jamie and Adam trailed the others as they climbed to the dig the next morning.

"The first thing we should look at is opportunity," Jamie said. "Who was in camp while we were swimming?"

"Sy didn't go," Adam said. "Or Hans."

"Right. Neither did Bonnie or the cook, but I think we can rule him out — he's been cooking at our digs for years."

"Okay. So the other time could have been at supper. Was anybody late?"

Jamie shrugged. "Just Lois. She had been writing up some stuff about wheat grass. She says their leaves curl up into a tube to conserve water when it's really dry, and she was all excited about actually seeing them do it."

"Anybody else?"

"No. I'm pretty sure nobody else was late enough to have had time to run from the acid bath to your camper, to the fossil hut, grab the stuff, ditch it." Jamie moved her fingers in a running motion as she spoke.

"So our list of suspects includes Hans, Sy, Bonnie, and Lois. Aw, nuts, Jamie, I don't believe it." Adam stamped his feet hard for a few steps.

"You're right, Adam. There has to be some other answer. But in the meantime we could start watching them. You know, do they look guilty, do they make excuses to be around camp when it's deserted, do they make any Freudian slips?"

"Like what?" He knew what a Freudian slip was, all right, a slip of the tongue that might reveal information about something a person was trying to repress, but he had never actually tried to identify one.

"Oh, you know, words like *rob*, *steal*, *guilt*, or *money* — stuff like that might creep into the conversation. We'll each take two of them."

"Yeah, okay, Doctor. I'll try. So which two are you going to psychoanalyze and which will be mine?"

"We'll take turns, okay? I'll be working with Bonnie, so I'll watch her today. You pay attention to the others, mostly Sy and Hans, I'd say. Lois doesn't seem like much of a suspect to me."

"Okay," Adam said. This was sounding a little simpler than he had expected. No sneaking around spying on people, no — his thoughts were interrupted by the words *fake egg*. "Pardon?" he asked.

"We're going to make a fake egg," Her voice was as matter-of-fact as if she were talking about baking cookies. "With rocks and plaster and stuff." Jamie was whispering, though Adam was sure there wasn't a creature within hearing distance, unless there happened to be a deer mouse hiding under the kinnickinnick. "And Herbie's going to help. He already knows about the missing stuff."

"What for?"

"Dad's locking up the real one in the Prowler, and we'll plant the fake one in the fossil shed."

"Pardon the stupid question, but if it's an inside job, won't the inside person know the difference?"

Jamie nodded. "Maybe. But if somebody's in a big hurry to grab it and run, they might not notice."

"I see." But he didn't really. Any member of the crew

would surely notice that the egg looked different.

Jamie seemed to read his thought. "We'll put it in a box with packing around it. And don't forget, it's most likely not an inside job, so the thief really won't know the difference."

Sy and Hans, and maybe Lois. Hans and Sy, and just possibly Lois. All Adam had to do was watch Sy and Hans. And Lois perhaps. He settled himself with his drawing pad and pretended he was concentrating on his work. The day was rather pleasant for a change — cooler than usual — and the voices matched the weather: soft murmurs, friendly chuckles.

He tried to keep his ears tuned to the conversation, but his attention was drawn to dinosaurs, as it always was when he had a sketchpad in front of him.

The movement of the land has left a higher area of good drainage halfway between the restless mountains and the giant sea — and here, for many generations, the Hypacrosaurs *have built their nests. The herd reaches the site, ready to mate and build again.*

Dozens of individuals have fallen prey to their meat-eating neighbours during the journey.

The mating begins. Huge bodies mill around. The males stomp, bellow, sniff the females. After two or three days of courtship, Hya's unlaid eggs are fertilized and the work begins.

Nest building.

The nesting ground is trampled and muddy. Hya chooses her spot carefully. It must be no closer to her neighbours than her own length so that she can move around to get food and water and lie beside the nest to guard it.

She digs up a mound of mud with her hind legs and hollows a bowl-shaped nest in the middle of it with her forelegs. Then she squats over the mound, using her forelegs to steady herself, and deposits her eggs. Ten of them, each twenty centimetres long and ten centimetres wide. She arranges the eggs in the nest with her snout. The pattern must be just right — a herringbone design.

Hya and her mate gather leaves and stalks and cover the nest carefully to help with the incubation. Then they rest.

The air is full of sounds: the suck of scooped-up mud, the plop of flying blobs of it, the grunts and thumps of mating, the straining sighs of egg laying, the rustle of foliage being gathered and spread over warm eggs.

Hya goes to the river to drink, then sits back on her hind legs with her broad, flat tail for support and stretches her neck to grasp needles and twigs. She moves about, lowers her fore limbs to the ground, and grazes on low-growing leaves and bushes.

When Hya hears warning cries, she turns and lumbers back to her nest, but she is too late. A Chirostenote *has sneaked in. It dashes away on its turkey-like legs holding one of Hya's eggs in its slender hands.*

"Rotten thief!" The words jerked Adam back to reality. Could that be a Freudian slip? And who had said it? He looked around. He must have said it to himself. The others were working silently, heads down, hands busy.

Hans spoke, putting on an exaggerated Scandinavian accent. "By yumpin' yimminy, chums. Take a gander at this." He was pointing to a chunk of rock that had been cut away from the pedestal. "A great example of cross-bedding and a perfect specimen for my thesis."

"What's your thesis called, Hans?" Lois asked.

Hans gazed at her with a smile. "I thought you'd never ask. It's called 'The Environment of Deposition of the Sediments Around the Dinosaur-Nesting Site on the Milk River Ridge.'"

"And in plain English that means?"

"What the formations tells us about the environment

when the rocks were laid down. See here?" He pointed at the wall of the excavation site. "That's called cross-bedding."

"You mean those layers going at angles?"

"Right. As you know, bones are usually found in fossil stream beds or flood plains where the sediment has covered them quickly. The cross-bedding shows the insides of ripples on the stream bed. You can tell how fast and in what direction the stream was flowing and even if the ripples formed in a stream or on a beach."

"You must have read the book," Lois said.

"I think he wrote the bloody book," Sy added.

Hans tucked the chunk of rock into his pack.

After lunch the day got hotter and everybody got quieter, but nobody made a Freudian slip, at least not one that Adam recognized.

At quitting time Al said, by way of an explanation to the others, "Adam wants to do a close-up sketch of the excavated site without any bodies in the way, and Jamie and Herbie will do some surface prospecting to keep him company."

They had fun making the egg. By three o'clock, the heat of the sun was partially screened by wispy clouds, the other people had left, and the "three musty steers," as Jamie called them, began their skullduggery.

"You're the stonemason and we're the plasterers," Jamie said to Adam.

She produced an aluminum pie plate she had spirited away from the cookhouse. Then she and Herbie gathered rocks of various shapes and sizes. Adam's job was to fit them into the pie plate as snugly as possible. Next, they wedged crumpled toilet tissue into the cracks, and Adam held the plate while Jamie and Herbie wound layer after layer of wet toilet tissue around, then covered it with burlap soaked in plaster.

"It's got to look like a real fossil," Jamie said, her tongue protruding from the corner of her mouth as she concentrated on smoothing the wet goop.

Adam's and Jamie's hands touched often as they manoeuvred the piece into different positions, and Adam began to be very aware of the feel of Jamie's fingers. There was something about her touch in the warmth of the hazy afternoon and the intimate space created by secretly shared activity that aroused his energy level. Was this the earthquake aftershock syndrome again?

Jamie took some time to admire their work. "Fantastic!" She stood at attention and saluted Herbie. "Phase one of poacher ensnarement plan successfully completed." She propped stones together to form a pinnacle and set the fake egg on it. "There. It should be dry in ten minutes or so. And then you can carry it down, Lieutenant. You don't have anything much in there." She pointed at Adam's pack.

"What do you mean, nothing much? I'll have you know I've got valuable works of art in here, not to mention the tools of the trade, Captain, sir." Adam did a caricature of a salute that resembled a thumbed nose.

Jamie glared at him with mock sternness. "You'll be in the brig if you keep up this kind of insubordination."

"Fine. As long as you're in there with me." The words were out before he'd had time to think.

Jamie poured water into a pail and started washing her hands. Adam put his hands in and flicked water at her. She giggled. Herbie joined the hand-washing game, and they splashed water at one another and congratulated themselves on the terrific egg they had "laid."

Then they found a shady spot and sat down.

"So what do you think, Herbie?" Adam asked. "About the missing fossils?" He hoped his nagging worry about the possibility that the others might think him guilty didn't show on his face.

"It's a puzzler." Herbie rubbed the side of his nose with his finger. "I'm really reluctant to entertain the idea that it could be one of the crew. Yet I don't see how it could possibly be an outsider. I keep hoping —" he folded his hands and leaned his elbows on his bent knees "— that the missing pieces will turn up."

"Wouldn't that be terrific if it was all just a mix-up and not thievery?" Jamie said. "But let's talk about something else. Something nice."

So Herbie told them about something that he considered nice, though probably not everyone would agree. In New Mexico he had seen rocks, some bigger than baseballs, that had actually been *inside* a dinosaur's digestive system, like gravel in a chicken's gizzard. "They found a fossil skeleton with a rock beside it and think that the animal died choking on a rock that was too big to swallow."

"Too bad there was nobody around to do the Heimlich manoeuvre," Adam said.

Herbie laughed. "Yeah. But even if you could get your arms around him from behind, and figure out which of his dozen or so ribs to put your hands under, I don't suppose he'd take too kindly to the squeezes."

"Blllup, blllup." Jamie made retching noises, grasped her midriff, leaned forward, put one hand to her mouth, and "spit out" a rock. Then she rubbed her stomach. "Boy, that feels better!"

"Hey!" Adam said. "A master of legerdemain. You

could make a career of that. Travel all over the world, make a fortune. The only prop you need is one rock."

"Great idea," Herbie said. "I'll be your manager. Let's see now." He scratched his chin. "We need a sales pitch."

"How about this?" Adam said, jumping to his feet. "Are you tired of the same old boring sideshows? Fire walking, sword swallowing, knife throwing, the usual ho-hum stuff?" He raised his chin and glanced disdainfully at his imaginary audience. "Of course, you are. Well, have we got something for you. Step right up and see the wonder girl. By a strange quirk of genetics, or possibly a new strain of virus, this young lady has the digestive system of a dinosaur. She swallows stones, that's right, folks, that's spelled s-t-o-n-e-s, to help digest her food. Sometimes the poor child gets carried away and tries to swallow a big one. Usually, I say, usually, she's able to expel the offending specimen without serious harm, but sometimes it can be a close call."

Herbie stood, spread his arms wide, and took up the spiel. "Unfortunately for us, ladies and gentlemen, scientists don't know if this malady is contagious, so why not be on the safe side? Be prepared. Before you get an irresistible urge to swallow stones, have a bottle of our handy-dandy Dinosaur Digestive Juice on hand. Only nine dollars and ninety-five cents. Guaranteed to protect you and your whole family."

"Oh-oh. Stop the show." Adam looked at Jamie. "I think our dinosaur kid is going to, yes, it's coming. She's going to — is she, isn't she, yes, she is! She going to regurgitate a stone right now!"

Jamie was laughing so hard she could hardly talk. "Hey, you two chauvinists, I don't like the sound of this. I do all the barfing and you make the bucks."

"Just relax and save your energy for important things,"

Adam said. "We'll handle the details." He offered his hand and pulled her to her feet. "And we'll even provide the stone."

"Well, thank you, sir," she said with a curtsy. "Your generosity is too much."

"No problem," Adam said.

CHAPTER 9

"That's a pretty good imitation," Al said, moving around the table in the Jamiesons' trailer to examine the fake egg from every angle.

And once he had marked it with his own distinctive printing style, even Jamie, Adam, and Herbie believed it could pass for the real thing.

"I'm going to get washed," Jamie said as they left the Prowler.

Adam thought she could use a wash, all right. She had untied her hiking boots and had shoved her red-striped wool socks down into the tops as far as they would go. The laces flapped, and several centimetres of clean white leg showed between the boots and the dirt-covered tan starting just above her ankles. Her face was streaked with dust, her red T-shirt was wet with perspiration under the arms, and her denim shorts were stained and wrinkled.

Not that he looked any better than she did. He carried a basin full of water from a plastic barrel beside the shower back to the camper, washed his face and hands, wet his hair, and combed it, peering into a little mirror that hung on the wall.

A little later Adam and Jamie were sitting in the shade drinking 7 Up and waiting for the supper gong. "What did you find out?" he asked her. "Any Freudian slips?"

She shook her head. "No, I didn't find out a single

solitary thing that we didn't already know. You?"

"Nothing. I must admit, though, I kind of lost focus at times. I had to pretend I was drawing, and the first thing I knew I really was drawing and then losing touch with the real world."

"Well, how about we trade? I'll watch Sy, and you can have Hans at the campfire tonight. That is, if they're both there."

It was Adam's turn to help with the kitchen cleanup, and Jamie had work to do in the fossil hut. Twilight had deepened to dusk by the time they headed for the campfire.

"Our work of art really looks authentic," she whispered to Adam. "Dad put it in a box with some foam chips so it looks like it's ready to be packed up when the museum people come."

Bonnie called as they approached, "Hi, sweeties. Look at the moon. Isn't that something else?"

"You bet your boots," Sy said as he stood and yawned. "A real humdinger. But I think I'll hit the sack."

Jamie shot Adam a knowing look, nodded in Sy's direction, and after a few seconds, followed him.

Adam sat beside Hans. Tonight the campfire gathering seemed subdued. Slim was singing a song about somebody with a blue-wing tattoo and a poor man's dream.

"Sounds like the student's theme song," Adam said. "'Poor Man's Dream.'"

"Yeah, man, tell me about it," Hans said. He started to drum his fingers on the table.

"It must be tough when you can't even earn bucks in the summer," Adam said.

"Yeah. I hitchhiked from Vancouver so I wouldn't have

to buy a bus ticket."

"Where the sun don't shine on a poor man's dream," Slim sang.

"How did you get your bike out?" Adam asked.

"Crated it and sent it by air. I know it sounds crazy, but I've got a thing about my bicycle. Separation anxiety, I guess. Where I go, my mountain bike goes."

It did sound a little weird. Hans wanted to have his bicycle at the dig so badly that he sent it in an airplane while he himself hitchhiked. Still, to each his own, Adam thought — like Sy and his oil wells and Bonnie and her stuffed kangaroos. Hans wanted to keep in shape for a big race, and a bicycle was functional. Without it Hans wouldn't be able to go on rides up and down steep bluffs.

Rides on bluffs. Hans liked to ride up and down the bluffs. Could there be another reason besides training for a race? Like fossil hiding or delivering fossils to an accomplice?

"How long does it take to get to the bluffs?" Adam asked.

"About twenty minutes on the bike," Hans said.

"I wouldn't mind going with you sometime."

"Sure." Hans stretched, stood, called "Good night, everybody," and left.

"Good night, sweetie," Bonnie said, waving. "See you in the a.m. I think I'm ready to call it quits, too. Sweet dreams, everybody." She cuddled Kanga and Roo to her chest.

Adam stayed for a few minutes longer and then left the campfire, hoping to intercept Jamie and talk about bicycle riding on bluffs, but she was nowhere to be seen.

Adam had to wait for seven hours to talk to Jamie. During that time, he slept fitfully, ate breakfast, made sandwiches for his lunch, took his frozen water bottle out of the fridge, and began climbing back up to Devil's Coulee.

It started out sensibly enough. Jamie told him everything she could remember about Sy, which wasn't much. He had gone into his trailer, closed the door, and lit a candle. A few minutes later the candle had been blown out, the trailer had creaked a few times, and that was about it.

"I found out that Hans had his bike sent out here by air freight," Adam said.

"Really?"

"Yeah, really. And what does he do with it?"

"Ride it." Jamie got the giggles. She hunched her shoulders and pantomimed holding handlebars and steering a bike. It would have been a wildly erratic ride, judging from her exaggerated movements.

"Hey, listen up, will you?" Adam said. "Where does he ride *to*?"

"Oh, around." Jamie laughed and steered her imaginary bicycle around in circles.

"He rides to those bluffs over there," Adam said irritably. "Good hiding places, wouldn't you think?" How could you talk sensibly to somebody who was being ridiculous?

"Oh, you mean maybe it could be something to do with smuggling?" She peered anxiously around like a sneaky cartoon character.

"Do you want to talk about this or not?" Adam demanded. He stopped walking, and Jamie ceased acting silly.

"So you think he could be stashing stuff there?" she asked.

"It's possible." Adam started to walk again, and she fell into step beside him.

"So what can we do about that?" Jamie asked. "We couldn't search every nook and cranny up there in a hundred years." She looked discouraged. "But you know what I was thinking? Sy keeps hanging around oil wells, and we could check them out."

"Right. And Lois wanders around in the dark a lot. I've seen her."

"Yeah, but she's just doing her thing. Watching the wheat grass grow. She wants to see it open and close itself."

"So she says," Adam said. "And what about Bonnie and her saskatoon patch? Maybe she's got a hiding place in a bush or something."

Jamie sighed. "Right. The plot thickens. Too many suspects and not enough clues. If it is an inside job."

"So where do we go from here?"

"Well, maybe we're trying too hard. Maybe we should just feed the questions in and let our subconscious take over for today."

"Sounds good to me," Adam said. He was anxious to concentrate on his sketching — do at least one more solid outline before he had to leave on Sunday. So he spent most of the day lost in communication with his sketchbook.

Jamie lingered behind the others as she and Adam started down the hill after the day's work. "We have to do some sleuthing before supper," she said.

"Where?" Adam asked.

"It would be nice to check out the bluffs, but that's a major job. We could poke around the oil wells and check out the saskatoon patch, though."

By three o'clock, Adam and Jamie were waiting to see what the others were planning to do so they could make some sleuthing decisions. Bonnie headed for the saskatoon patch, Hans went off on his bike, and Sy started walking across the field toward the nearest oil well.

"His hat!" Adam cried, grabbing Jamie's hand.

She frowned. "Huh? What are you talking about?"

"Sy's hat. He never takes his hat off. Why do you suppose that is?"

"Don't ask me. It's another security blanket, I guess." She flipped her hand backward in a dismissive manner.

Adam was excited. "But what if, now get this, Jamie, my girl, what if his hat has a false compartment? I bet he could fit quite a few small fossils in between his head and the crown. Who would ever suspect a Panama hat?"

"I wonder …" Jamie stared at the ground. "I don't know about Sy. He seems so harmless, but he does have a lot of stuff in his private collection. Wouldn't that be weird? We have to find out. One of us has to get a good look inside that hat." She stuck out her lower lip and blew a puff of air up toward her bangs. "Plus we have to investigate Hans somehow. Maybe we should poke around a bit before he gets back. I wonder what's in that canvas bag beside his tent."

"He said it was dirty laundry."

"Ha! Laundry, eh? I've heard that one before. Some people I know smuggled cigarettes across the border in a baby's diaper bag. Come on, let's go have a look."

"But, Jamie, we can't just go over and start hauling stuff out of Hans's bag like that." He snapped his fingers.

"Not like that," she said, snapping her own fingers. "Like this." She put her hand beside her leg, gazed around innocently, and rubbed her thumb across her index finger. "I'll just feel around inside it."

"I don't think we should."

"Adam, don't you understand? Stealing fossils is as bad

as tomb raiding. You have to fight fire with fire, and we won't be doing any harm. We'll just be checking out Hans's dirty laundry, if that's what it is. You can be the lookout."

So Adam was whistling and strolling along the road with his hands in his pockets while Jamie was hunched down with her hand inside the bag when Lois appeared out of nowhere. Adam whistled a long, sharp note.

Jamie glanced up, smiled, and waved. "Hi, Lois.

Lois stopped in her tracks and stared at Jamie.

"It's okay," Jamie said. "We just want to borrow Hans's magnifying glass, and I think he said it was in this bag."

Lois frowned. "Oh, is that what you're doing? I wondered. Here, you can have mine." She opened her fossil bag and handed the glass to Jamie.

"Thanks, Lois. We want to have a look at something Adam discovered, and I can't find my own glass." She closed Hans's bag and shot Adam a look.

Lois strolled away slowly, shaking her head and peering at the ground.

"That was a pretty close call," Adam said.

Jamie grinned. "Yeah, wasn't it? Don't you think I did a good job of fooling her?"

"You did if she was really fooled. I'm not so sure about that, though."

"Oh, Adam, there you go again. You worry too much. At a dig like this people borrow each other's stuff all the time. It's like open season, especially on things we get free. Hammers, picks, and brushes are a different matter — some people don't like to loan them. But most do."

"And you didn't find anything."

"No, but I didn't get to the bottom of the bag. Maybe we'll get another chance."

"And maybe Hans will notice his laundry isn't the way he left it," Adam said. If that was being stodgy, so be it. There was such a thing as common sense, not to mention natural consequences. He would try to explain that to Jamie when the circumstances seemed more favourable.

CHAPTER 10

Adam was standing behind the camper where he was hidden from view, practising the moves to Embrace Tiger, Return to Mountain. He had done his warm-ups, the deep breaths, shaking himself, letting the tension go, moving very slowly, stretching his arms over his head, trying to get a sense of balance. "Let your spine be like a willow," his tai chi book said. He concentrated on allowing the yang space of his body to be aware of the yin space around him — letting his body rest in space, trying to capture both the feeling of letting go and the sensation of awareness. *Don't try too hard,* he kept reminding himself. *Find your centre. Let your body stretch and move and return to your centre. Keep your weight centred between your legs, ready to move in any direction.*

Jamie appeared.

"Hi," he said.

"Is that judo?" she asked.

Adam shook his head. "It's tai chi, but it's the same preliminary training used in all the martial arts."

"Could you teach me some of it? Please?"

Adam read her some passages from his book, and she concentrated on his instructions.

"Do it a little more slowly," he said. "Follow your breath. Exhale on the down movements. Inhale as you move up. That's it. *Slo-o-owly.*"

"Like, wow! It must take a lot of practice to be able to

hold the positions the way you do. Maybe I could borrow your book sometime?"

"For sure," Adam said.

Jamie lay on the grass, and he sat beside her. She was wearing a turquoise shirt, and her eyes were aquamarine. They reminded Adam of a mountain lake.

"Okay, the thing with Hans's pack didn't work out quite right, but now we have to see Sy's hat, right?" Jamie closed her eyes.

"I guess so, but I sure as heck don't know how to go about that."

"I've got a plan."

"You have?" Adam had mixed emotions. He fervently hoped her plan wouldn't involve too many little white lies, or big black ones.

"The plan is …" Her voice was low and conspiratorial. "First, I'll knock on his door in the middle of the night and tell him I'm scared. Then I'll get him to come outside with me." She sat up, stretched her legs straight, and reached for her ankles with both hands.

"Then what?"

She turned her head sideways and peered up at him from the vicinity of her knees. "Once I get him out I'll persuade him to go with me to look for a burglar and then you go in and do a quick search."

"Is that all?" Adam jerked his shoulders back. "Just a quick look, eh? In somebody else's camper in the middle of the night? Thanks a heck of a bunch. I don't *think* so."

"Come on, Adam. Do you want to solve this crime or not?"

"Sure I do, but you've got to be nuts. That's the most hare-brained scheme I've ever heard." Luring Sy out of his camper, expecting he would fall for her story and not want to wake up everybody else in camp if she was afraid of an intruder — the plan was crazy. But Jamie looked as excited as a kid at a Santa Claus parade. "Couldn't we just check out the oil well instead?" Adam asked hopefully. "We haven't done that yet."

She shook her head. "I want to follow up on the hat lead before he gets a chance to ditch the stuff somewhere."

"*If* there's any stuff to ditch. Come on, Jamie, we'll be in real trouble if we're not careful. At least I will." It was fine for her, but he could be out on his ear in a second, banned from dinosaur digs forever.

"Well, I'm going to do it with or without you." Jamie leaned back and rubbed her shoulder blades against the camper. "I'm going to knock on his door and ask him if I can hide in there because somebody's chasing me."

Obviously, there was no stopping her.

Adam had thought he was willing to go to great lengths to avoid being stodgy, but this was going a lot farther than he had ever imagined. He sighed, glanced at Jamie, shook his head, then nodded and said, "Okay." One thing he was sure about: he would be very glad if they did find the real thief so the others couldn't suspect him.

There was no campfire after supper. Al and Jamie left to do some shopping, so they said, but their real purpose was to meet some people from the Royal Tyrrell Museum and deliver the real egg and some of the more unusual fossils into safe hands. They would stop at a camera shop where they could get one-hour service, because Al had two films to be developed, including the time-sequence one, Bonnie had one, and Mike had one.

Adam felt a mixture of guilt and relief when he saw

Hans looking perfectly natural and unconcerned as he handed over his dirty laundry tied up in a pillowcase. It was to be dropped off at a jiffy laundry near the camera shop.

Everybody else was busy — cleaning and classifying specimens, reading, writing in field notebooks, talking about plans for the weekend, tidying up the campsite.

Adam read his tai chi manual and then worked on adding detail to his sketches. By 10:00 p.m., Jamie and her father still weren't back. Maybe they had decided to stay in Vulcan or Lethbridge overnight. He went to bed convinced that Jamie had forgotten her insane plan.

Jamie hadn't forgotten her plan, though. Adam was awakened by a tap on his window at 1:00 a.m.

"Hide under his camper," she whispered.

Adam crawled under Sy's camper. He heard a quiet tap on Sy's door and Jamie's breathless voice saying, "Sy, I'm scared." Then everything was quiet until the silence was broken by another, louder tap. "Sy, can you come and help me?"

There was a bump, followed by shuffles and the sound of the door opening. Then Sy's surprised voice cried, "Jamie! What the devil?" He was interrupted by Jamie's frantic whispers.

All Adam could understand was the occasional word such as *scared*. Then there was a low mumbling, and he caught the words *light* and *path*." Finally, there were more whispers, followed by two sets of stealthy footsteps.

Adam crawled to the edge of the camper and watched them scurry along the path. He was both relieved and dismayed by what he saw. Sy was wearing his Panama hat. In the middle of the night?

He was relieved that he didn't have to sneak into the camper. Jamie would be disappointed, but wasn't this proof positive there was something very important about that hat? Why had she continued with the plan once she saw him wearing it?

"Who knows?" Adam muttered to himself as he crawled out from his hiding place. He crawled too fast. His shoulder caught on the exhaust pipe with a ripping sound and a loud, tinny rattle. Adam wiggled the last few feet and stood. Then he heard a knock on Sy's door and Herbie's voice. "Sy, are you all right?"

Adam froze.

"Sy, it's me, Herbie. Are you okay?"

All was quiet. Herbie walked around the camper toward the window.

"It's okay," Adam said. "It's just me."

Herbie stared at Adam's sleeve, which was half ripped out of the armhole. "Is Sy okay?"

"Yeah, but he's not here."

"Where is he?"

"Um …" Adam's first impulse was to make up an excuse, but he decided to tell the truth. "We wanted to see the inside of Sy's hat. He never takes it off, and we thought maybe he had a contraption for hiding fossils in it. So Jamie got him to go out so I could snoop. You understand?" He gazed at Herbie anxiously.

Herbie did seem to understand. "Well, did you get a look at it?"

"No. Sy had it on when he left."

"Really? That's strange. But here they come. We better move out to the road."

Sy and Jamie approached at a leisurely walk. "It's okay,"

Jamie said. "I guess it was just a deer. I thought somebody was hiding there beside the path. Scared me half to death. Thanks, Sy. Sorry to disturb your sleep." She patted his arm.

"S'okay," Sy said.

Just then Bonnie arrived. "Haven't you guys been to bed yet?"

The whole scene was ludicrous beyond belief. Adam shook his head and blinked. These people were all serious-minded science types?

Sy, in striped pajamas, rubber boots, and a Panama hat, was picking spear grass out of his pant leg. Herbie, wearing boxer shorts and unlaced hiking boots, was gazing up at the sky with his arm outstretched. "Satellite," he said. Bonnie, wearing a pink dressing gown, was hugging her stuffed toys. Adam's own T-shirt sleeve was hanging by a thread.

Jamie pointed from one to the other and began to giggle. "I'm sorry. It was my fault. I thought I saw somebody in the bushes." She was laughing now with her hand over her mouth. Her shoulders were shaking.

Hans arrived wearing a yellow rain slicker, which sent Jamie into more paroxysms of laughter. Soon everybody was laughing with her. They tried to do it quietly.

"Shh, don't wake up the whole camp," they whispered at one another, then laughed all the harder.

Jamie's story about heading for the toilets and seeing what she thought was a person lurking beside the path, and then deciding it must have been a deer, seemed to make sense. More or less.

And all for the sake of a peek inside Sy's hat, which he had worn the whole time.

"Why did you go ahead with it when you saw he was

wearing it?" Adam asked as they walked back through the compound.

"I don't know. The plan was already made. I had to say something. And I thought maybe I could accidentally bump it off his head. It just didn't work out, that's all." She clasped her hands behind her neck and rotated her elbows.

"Well, one thing for sure, we know that hat's pretty darn important to Sy."

"Too bad. Number one plan didn't work very well, and number two plan didn't work at all. Hey, we can still check out the oil well."

Adam sighed. "Now?"

"Sure, why not? I'm not tired, are you?"

"You're serious? You want to snoop around an oil well at —" he glanced at his watch "— 1:28 a.m.?"

"You got it," Jamie said. "It won't take long. Grab a shirt and I'll meet you behind the fossil hut."

"Okay ..."

The oil well pump was enclosed in a four-metre-by-four-metre area surrounded by a chain-link fence. There was a sign on the locked gate: PROPERTY OF SHELL OIL. NO ADMISSION. TRESPASSERS WILL BE PROSECUTED TO THE FULL EXTENT OF THE LAW.

"So that's it," Adam said, shining his flashlight toward the base of the pump. "You can't see anything much from here."

"So then we have to get in," Jamie said with a shrug.

"Jamie! You are kidding, aren't you? What does that say?" He pointed at the sign.

"Aw, don't be such a wimp. We aren't going to do anything wrong. We're just going to have a look. What's more important — to catch a fossil thief or obey every picky little rule they come up with?"

"But they're a big powerful company, and we're just —"

Jamie was already climbing over the fence, so how could Adam do anything except follow?

They crawled around on their hands and knees and searched the ground inside the fence, poking under grass, raking loose gravel with sharp rocks.

"I wish we had a wrench," Jamie said. "I think if we could loosen one of the bolts on this concrete thing we could lift this metal plate up a few centimetres."

"For God's sake, Jamie, we can't tamper with — shh, I think I hear an engine."

Jamie listened. "It's probably just a car on the road. Sound travels at night, you know."

Adam stood and looked around. "I don't see any lights."

"Maybe it's a plane. Come on, let's get on with it."

"What's going on here?" The loud voice slammed out of the darkness, and Adam and Jamie were pinned in the beam of a powerful light.

Adam blinked and stared.

"It's not the way it seems, sir," Jamie said. "We're just looking for, um, something."

"Sure you are," the voice said. "You're looking for something on your hands and knees in the dark on private property. Let me guess now. Could it be, say, mushrooms, or gold, or did you figure you could steal oil? Or plant a bomb? Get out of there!"

They heard the clank of metal as the gate was unlocked and the flashlight beam beckoned them through it.

"No, sir," Jamie said politely.

They could now see two men dressed in uniforms.

"We can explain everything," Jamie said, the words tumbling out. "We work on the dinosaur dig right over there.

And somebody's stealing fossils. So we thought they were hiding them here. We just wanted to have a look for fossils. That's all." She raised her hands, palms up.

"Do you actually think we're going to buy that?" the man doing the talking asked. "Shine the light on them one at a time, Gil."

Gil moved the light slowly up and down Adam first, then Jamie.

"See if there's a package or anything suspicious inside the fence."

"Nothing here that I can see, Frank," Gil said after a few seconds.

"So what do you think that sign means?" Frank demanded.

"It means people shouldn't go in there unless it's something really important, like catching fossil thieves," Jamie said firmly, head held high, hands on her hips.

"Man, oh, man," Frank said, "where did you learn to read? You've got to be the brassiest girl I've ever run into." He shook his head. "Get out the book, Gil. We'll get their vital statistics and check them out with whoever's in charge." He nodded in the direction of the camp.

Jamie announced her name, address, birth date, and next of kin as if she were expecting to be congratulated for being who she was.

After Adam politely answered questions about himself, the two of them were led to a Jeep parked behind a hill.

"How did you know we were here?" Jamie asked as she climbed in.

"What do you think we are — a bunch of idiots?" Frank growled. "We've got surveillance on all the rigs. You never know what kind of kooks will crawl out of a hole in the ground and get us out to the middle of the desert in the middle of the night." He continued to mumble as they drove across the pasture and parked beside the Jamiesons' trailer.

During the ride, Adam had tried to imagine what Al's reaction would be. Anger? Disbelief? Worry about the consequences of his daughter's and her "old friend's" foolhardiness? And exactly what did "prosecuted to the full extent of the law" mean? What was the full extent of the law?

Al, who was adjusting sweatpants that he had pulled on over his pajamas, met them at the door.

"This your daughter, sir?" Frank asked.

"Yes." Al's face was immobile. Only his eyes moved.

"And is her friend here called Adam Zapo-something?"

"Yes."

"And do they both work on some kind of dinosaur deal here?"

"Yes."

"Well, sir, we picked up your daughter and this young man for trespassing on Shell Oil property out in the field." He jerked his thumb over his shoulder. "They gave us a line about looking for fossils."

"Please come inside," Al said.

They went inside, sat down, and heard Jamie's whole story. When she was finished, Al said, shaking his head, "Jamie, Jamie …"

"I left a note just like I always do, Dad."

Al glanced at a scrap of paper held by a clothes peg that was attached to the wall beside the door, nodded, and turned to the guards. "It's true. We've had some fossil thefts. So what's your next move? Do you intend to prosecute?"

"It's our duty to report this," Frank said loftily. "This is a serious offence. Just in case you hadn't heard, the fine is five thousand dollars. Each!"

Jamie gasped, Al sucked in an audible breath, and Adam's jaw dropped open.

Frank seemed satisfied that his message had had the impact he wanted, then spoke directly to Al. "If you'll vouch for the two of them and keep them out of trouble, we might consider not proceeding at this point in time. I said at this point in time." He glared at Jamie and Adam in turn. "You better watch your step, or we'll throw the book at you."

"Sure," Jamie said. "That's exactly what we intend to do, isn't it, Adam?"

Adam hoped it was exactly what she intended to do, but he wouldn't have placed a bet on it.

CHAPTER 11

"Jamie, you really did go too far this time," Al said with a sigh when the men had left. "We have to be careful about our reputations. You know that."

"I know, Dad." Jamie patted his back. "I got carried away. I'm sorry."

"I'm sorry, too," Adam said. "It was my fault just as much as Jamie's, and there's nothing I can do to change what's already happened, but I give you my word of honour that I'll be more careful if you'll let me stay. I mean, I'll be careful, anyway, even if you don't let me stay. But I sure hope you'll let me stay. This is the most exciting thing I've ever ..." He stopped for breath and realized he was babbling. The best thing he could do at that point, he decided, was to shut up.

"Don't blame Adam, Dad," Jamie said. "It was my fault."

"No!" Adam protested. "It was my fault just as much as yours, maybe more."

"Okay, okay," Al said. "I don't need to hear an argument about whose fault it was. We'll forget it for the time being and hope we don't get a nasty surprise in the form of a summons for a court appearance. Five thousand dollars each. Any more of this kind of thing and there'll be serious consequences! You hear?"

"Yeah, sure, Dad. Hey, I've got an idea," Jamie said in a burst of excitement.

"Oh, no! Not already." Al held his head in his hands. "What is it this time?"

"Don't worry. It's perfectly legal, Dad. This is what I think. If Sy's doing it, he couldn't add the fossils to his private collection. He'd get caught for sure. It has to be for money. And whether it's Sy or somebody else, if it is an inside job, then the stuff has to be stashed somewhere and delivered to a buyer. It's for sure it would have to be sent out of the country. The easiest way to get it out of the country would be at the border crossing at Coutts. Right?" She looked at Adam.

"I guess so."

"Then you and I, my dear Watson, will leave early on Saturday and ride down that way. We'll pretend we're going to Writing-on-Stone Provincial Park. Maybe we'll get lucky and pick up a clue. Deal?"

"Okay with me," Adam said.

"Okay, Dad?"

"Um, I'll think about it. Just be careful you don't — oh, never mind." Al's shoulders sagged, and he turned away. "At least stay together. Promise me that much."

Adam had mixed emotions as he headed to bed. Al must think he was an idiot. It was a bad scene, no matter how you looked at it. He and Jamie had taken a chance that could have resulted in bad publicity for the whole project. But there was a plus side. Al had said that Adam and Jamie were to stay together on Saturday, so that must mean he trusted Adam to some degree. It was small comfort.

The mood was buoyant at breakfast the next morning. People chattered about the importance of the work they were doing and the international reputation the dig was receiving. Then

Al came in, a worried expression creasing his face. "Could I have your attention, please?" he asked loudly.

"Hey, listen up, guys," Mike barked.

"Al wants to make an announcement," Herbie announced, tapping a coffee cup with a teaspoon.

The hubbub subsided.

"I'm afraid we've got trouble," Al said.

A ripple of indrawn breaths and whispered anxiety moved around the room.

"I hate to have to tell you this, but we have some fossils missing."

Gasps of disbelief were followed by incredulous murmurs.

"I think it's only fair that you know, since we wouldn't have had any excavated fossils if all of you hadn't done such hard work." He waved his arm around the room. "Unfortunately, a lot of smaller items have disappeared, and this morning the egg was gone."

There were more gasps.

Al shrugged. "We don't know how or when. Maybe there's another key to the gate out there. Anything's possible. Anyway, I'd like to ask that you all be extra vigilant. I've arranged for Phil and Joe from the Royal Tyrrell to come and get anything of value. In the meantime I'd appreciate it if you would all go back up to Devil's Coulee and carry on as usual."

Lois raised her hand. "But, Al, we're almost sure to get another egg out today. What do we do about that? We'll have to guard it with our lives."

"Only until we can get it transferred to the museum," Al said. "We'll have a meeting on Sunday night and try to decide what to do."

"Why wait until then?" Mike asked.

"Because I think it would do us all good to get a little distance on the situation. Have a weekend break, do something different, try to remember anything you might have seen or heard that could provide a clue."

This would be Adam's last day at the egg site, at least for this year and maybe forever, though he was reluctant to give that idea serious consideration.

Everybody was obviously trying to act normal, but there was a kind of slow-motion lethargy about their actions, and was there something else? Were there suspicious glances being directed his way? Were they whispering his name and wondering? Lois seemed to be her normal matter-of-fact self, but how could she not be suspicious now about his and Jamie's snooping in Hans's bag? Jamie would be okay — she was the boss's daughter — but the so-called artist kid could have put her up to something.

Adam's emotions were on a roller coaster. He was worried, and glad, and hopeful, and sad, and despondent by turns.

He was sad at the thought of leaving and maybe never seeing Jamie again. He was sad at the breach of trust these people were obviously struggling with. He was sad about the missing fossils and the thought that there were people who were willing to steal, lie, and ruthlessly take advantage of others for the sake of money.

He was glad he had met Jamie. He was glad he had some good nest site drawings and some reasonably good *Hypacrosaur* sketches for his portfolio. He was glad — in fact, he was excited — about the idea of going off tomorrow with Jamie for the whole day. Maybe they would make it as far as the park. The idea intrigued him — works of art, pictographs and petroglyphs, made centuries before using only rocks and clay. Would any of them resemble dinosaurs?

And he was glad they had fashioned the fake dinosaur egg and that the real one was safe.

He was worried about being suspected of stealing, and the possibility of a huge fine, and Al's opinion of him, and what Lois might be thinking. Quit! He shuddered and shook himself. This was going nowhere. Concentrate on the world out there, he told himself firmly.

He gazed around, trying to anchor the scene so clearly in his mind that he would be able to pull up every detail from memory. Had he really believed just five days ago that this place was barren and ugly?

The morning air was still cool and damp, and a herd of pronghorn grazed in the distance. Little blurs of movement dotted the eroded patches — rabbits or gophers? A hawk was a tiny speck in the immense prairie sky.

The colours were intense — the deep delphinium-blue of the sky, the golden shimmer of the wheat grass, the stratified ochres and greys of the coulee walls, the rust and sand-castle-brown of the hoodoos, the deep green of the kinnick-innick accentuated with red berries. It was spellbinding, and Adam felt a deep sense of reverence and love for this land. It had been lush and verdant once when the dinosaurs were here, but more beautiful than this? Impossible.

He stared at the rocks beneath his feet. Hya had walked in this very place, guarding her nest, gathering food, dying, fulfilling her destiny. What was his destiny? What could he do more than he was doing now to connect with those ancient creatures and, in fact, all of the different forms of life that had inhabited this planet? Draw them, paint them, preserve their memory in the only way he knew how, as the ancient peoples had done at Writing-on-Stone Provincial Park. Adam imagined a ten-kilometre-long wall hung with his paintings — all the various life forms that had ever lived. He got out his sketchpad and started to work.

By lunchtime, team spirits had improved. For one thing, another egg was in the final stages of excavation and would be safely out of the nest no later than two o'clock. For another, people reminded one another of the treasures still buried in the rocks. There were at least five more nests intact, with no danger of them being stolen.

It had been an outsider, they agreed. Somebody had managed to get in without being seen. He must have eavesdropped on the campfire in order to know about Adam's amber and Jamie's tooth collection, then sneaked back in when the camp was quiet — Sy sleeping, Bonnie picking berries, Hans off on his bicycle, the cook away for groceries, the rest of them at the dam. The thief had come back more than once; the stolen egg was obviously a nighttime job. So all it meant was extra vigilance from now on.

The second egg was just as beautiful as the first and seemed even more precious now that its predecessor was gone, or so everyone else thought.

Al took another series of time-lapse photos, Bonnie snapped several shots of the group gathered around their treasure, and Adam made a close-up sketch of the egg. They talked about what they were going to do for the weekend as they gathered up tools and stored the leftover water in a barrel.

Adam turned and waved a slow farewell as they started down from the coulee. "I'll be back next year, Hya. If I have to crawl on my hands and knees, I'll be here." He whispered the words silently.

The rivers, choked with debris from the exploding mountain, rise. The air is thick with dust. The smell of sulphur is sickening. Hya huddles beside her nest. Warning bellows and frightened calls sound muted and distant to her ears.

Water laps around her feet. It begins to trickle into the nest.

The menace creeps higher and higher. The nursery blanket of leaves and branches begins to float, then drift away in shreds of rotting vegetation. She hunches beside her wet, muddy eggs.

The juveniles are the first to go. They stampede, run to their mothers for protection, but the parents push them away. The hatchlings and eggs have priority now. The juveniles run from danger they do not understand, splashing frantically through the water, looking for higher ground. Many are swept off their feet by a sudden surge of water; they begin to swim desperately.

Soon the males, and finally the other females, lumber away through the water. Bodies of newborn hatchlings tumble past, lodge on debris, then float again. The only sound now is the splash and trickle of water.

Hya keeps her vigil. She coughs and gags on the ash-laden air, hunkers down in water up to her knees. The water recedes, and still Hya crouches. Finally, exhausted and starving, she collapses silently into a heap. Her body lies heavy and still beside her mud-filled nest.

The land looks different — covered with a layer of silt, strewn with the bodies of dead animals. Predators gorge. Some of the Hypacrosaurs — adults and surviving juveniles — return to their home on the delta. But there will never be another nesting season for the gentle duckbills. The environmental change is inexorable. The large creatures cannot adapt.

"There has to be something we're missing," Jamie said as they walked back to camp. "What have we done so far?" She counted on her fingers. "Tried to check out Hans's laundry. The oil well thing didn't quite work. There could be stuff hidden there. We tried to check the inside of Sy's hat, but I'm beginning to have my doubts about that. Sure, the small stuff would fit inside it, but not the egg." She held up a fourth finger. "We haven't had a look at Bonnie's saskatoon patch. We should do that as soon as we get back, while she's busy having her shower and stuff."

So they did that.

The saskatoon grove was an oasis of rustling leaves, cool air, and the smell of ripe berries. No wonder Bonnie liked picking saskatoons.

"What are we looking for?" Adam asked.

"Just a good hiding place," Jamie said. "Maybe there's a hollow tree trunk, or a bird's nest, whatever."

"Okay, you look up and I'll look down and then we'll do a vice versa." Adam began to wander slowly through the grove. There were pathways where the grass was flattened, and larger trampled areas under some of the trees.

A pile of leaves in the middle of a clump of saplings caught his attention, and he got down on his hands and knees and crawled under the low branches to have a closer inspection. Brushing aside the leaves, he shook his head in disbelief. Purple berries filled the narrow depression. What was this all about? Who would keep a stash of saskatoon berries? He called Jamie.

"That's weird," she said, hands on her hips as she peered down at Adam. "Somebody must have put them here, but why?"

"Search me. Maybe Bonnie has some kind of a saskatoon fetish — a hoard of berries makes her feel secure, like her stuffed toys." Adam sat back on his heels.

"We have to talk to her after supper," Jamie said.

"I guess so …"

CHAPTER 12

By the time he'd had his shower, Adam's body was clean, but his brain was in turmoil. Visions of stolen fossils, a fake fossil, dirty laundry, saskatoon berries, stuffed kangaroos, and a Panama hat flashed in his head like a slide show gone crazy. And then there was the trespassing — a five-thousand-dollar fine was still possible. And the worst thought of all: what if the thief wasn't found and the thefts stopped when he left? In all the years Al Jamieson had supervised digs there had never been a single thing stolen until Adam had appeared on the scene. Things couldn't possibly be any worse.

Come on, Adam, calm down, he said to himself. *Put your energy into something useful instead of moaning. Do some tai chi.*

He moved around to the back of the camper and started with his breathing. *Calm and deep. Clear your mind. Make it work. Don't try too hard. Feel your centre.*

Something unusual attracted his attention. A scrap of white was caught in the door of a small storage area near the back of the camper. Funny he hadn't noticed it before. It was probably just a piece of newspaper. He tried the handle, pulled the door open, and things did get worse. Inside, besides some crumpled newspaper, was something he recognized — the fake egg!

Now what? This made the case against him even more incriminating. Would anyone believe that somebody else had put it there? Not very likely. His ears buzzed and his stomach churned. For a second or two he almost believed he *had* done it. His first impulse was to ditch the thing. But then he heard his father's voice. *Don't panic. Take your time. Think things through.* Maybe this was a blessing in disguise. The thief would surely be back for the egg before tomorrow morning when everybody left for the weekend.

He would stay inside the camper and watch. No, that wouldn't work. Jamie would come looking for him if he didn't turn up for supper. He decided to tie a thread to the latch on the storage compartment, go to supper, and if anybody was missing or left early, he would make some excuse and leave. If the thread wasn't broken when he got back, he would be doubly sure the thief would be making a nighttime visit. All he had to do was stay awake, watch, and listen. He got some thread from the small sewing kit his mother had insisted he bring and tied it in place.

Supper seemed to last forever.

Sy told a long story about oil wells. About a big find and being in the doghouse looking at the geolograph to see how fast and how deep the drill was going.

"But why, sweetie?" Bonnie asked. She was sitting between him and Herbie. "Why were you in the doghouse?"

Sy lowered his head and peered at her over the top of his glasses. "You must understand, my dear, that's what the work shack was called and that's where the geolograph was. And then the toolpusher —" He stopped when Bonnie interrupted him with a hand on his arm and a questioning look. "Oh, sorry. The toolpusher is the guy in charge of the crews." And on and on it went. About a rig burning out and how he had worked on Leduc Number One when he was just a kid.

Adam decided he had to tell Jamie about his plan. He might need somebody to confirm his story later if he didn't catch the thief, or he might be knocked unconscious inter-cepting the person and nobody would know why, or …

"Yeah, okay," Jamie said. "Sounds like a good idea, but do you think you can stay awake all night?"

"Sure," Adam said. "I drank four cups of coffee."

"So are we still going to talk to Bonnie?"

"Definitely."

Bonnie was on the lounge chair in front of her tent writing in a notepad when Jamie called. "We're going to have a Coke. Want one?"

"For sure, sweetie," Bonnie said. "That would be super. I'll be right over."

"Great. We're going to watch the sunset by Adam's camper. Bring a chair."

Bonnie didn't bring a chair, but she did bring Kanga and Roo and a folding stool. She pushed Roo down so that the tip of his nose poked over the top of the pouch, pat-ted his head, and put Kanga on the ground. "Thanks," she said, reaching for the Coke Jamie handed her, then sat on the stool.

Jamie was sitting on the camper step, and Adam was lying on his side on the grass, leaning on one elbow, his hand supporting his head. He sat up slowly and stared, en-tranced at the scene before him. Iridescent shifts of colour bewitched his senses. Jamie and Bonnie were both breath-takingly beautiful. He was overwhelmed with a passion of longing and regret. His eyes felt hot. For the first time in his life he wished he had learned a different kind of art, stud-ied the old masters like Titian and Botticelli. He ached to paint these young women — bare arms and legs glowing in the marigold sunshine, long dark hair rippling with glints of bronze, copper, and chestnut.

Bonnie and Jamie looked at each other, nodded, and smiled. Adam could see their mouths forming words, but he was oblivious to their meaning. He shivered, swallowed the lump in his throat, and reached for his Coke.

A question hung in the air.

Bonnie was speaking. "Yeah, I've got an older brother, two older sisters, and a younger sister. She's a real sweetie."

"Aw, I wish I had a sister," Jamie said. "What do your brother and sisters do? Are any of them paleontologists?"

Bonnie answered slowly. "No. None of them had a chance to go to college. My dad had a corner store, you know the kind — open from seven in the morning until midnight and everybody had to help. So they didn't have time to study or anything." She stared at Kanga.

"Wow! They must be really proud of you."

"For sure. It's a status thing, you know? Especially for my parents. I'm third-generation Canadian. My grandparents were white Russian — chased out of Ukraine." Bonnie's usually animated face changed and became frightened and sad. Her eyes focused up and to the right as though she were summoning from her own memory the anguish of her ancestors' flight from their homeland. She sat very straight with her hands clasped tightly in her lap.

Jamie reached over and put her hand on top of Bonnie's clenched ones. "It must have been hard for them."

Bonnie nodded, glanced at Jamie, and tried to smile, but there were tears in her eyes.

For a moment the only sounds were those of distant voices and bird calls.

Bonnie sniffled, pulled a tissue from her pocket, and blew her nose. "Would you believe that now there are over thirty descendants and I'm the first one to make it to university?"

She unclenched her hands and leaned back. "And my mom and dad give every single one of them a blow-by-blow. 'Bonnie's grades, Bonnie's professors, Bonnie's dinosaur dig, Bonnie's college friends.' I'm glad they're proud of me, but it's heavy."

"Sounds like it," Jamie said.

They sipped their Cokes for several minutes without speaking.

"Have any of you ever been back to Ukraine?" Jamie asked finally.

Bonnie shook her head. "No money. We just barely made a go of it. My dad sunk everything into the business."

"More power to you," Jamie said. "Managing to get it together to study paleontology."

"My folks helped as much as they could, and I got bursaries and loans, the usual thing. Thank God I've only got one more year to go, then maybe I can start making some bucks. I want Susie to have a chance. She's a smart kid, and I'm going to pay for whatever kind of education she wants." Bonnie pressed her lips together.

"Susie's your little sister?" Jamie asked.

Bonnie nodded and stood. "Yeah. Thanks for the Coke. See you later." She gathered up her stool and her stuffed animals, started to leave, then turned back. "Your dad said there was a bike under your trailer that I can borrow."

"That's right," Jamie said.

"I want to go to Writing-on-Stone Park tomorrow. Take pictures of Kanga and Roo with the petroglyphs to give to the uncle I got them from. He's an amateur anthropologist."

"Sure. I'll leave the bike beside your tent," Jamie said.

"Thanks, sweetie. I could hitchhike, but I'd rather ride." Bonnie waved goodbye.

"Well, so much for asking Bonnie about saskatoons, right?" Jamie said.

"Right," Adam said quietly. "The best-laid plans. That girl is sure carrying a load of anxiety under that bright and ditzy front."

"For sure. Poor Bonnie. It must be hard to think that thirty people are looking over your shoulder while you're studying." Jamie jumped up and shook the last few drops from her Coke can. "I'm glad we talked to her, though. It helps you understand where people are coming from when you hear their stories."

Adam was startled to realize that he had almost forgotten about his own predicament, but it came back with a vengeance. He tried to concentrate on his drawings, but all he could think about was the camper storage area and the impossibility of trying to come up with a reasonable explanation for its contents. His only hope was to catch the thief red-handed, but even that probably wouldn't work. It would be his word against somebody else's, and everybody on the crew except Jamie would certainly be inclined to believe that he was the guilty one. Newcomers and strangers were always blamed when things went wrong, weren't they?

He wandered around, keeping the camper within view, and tried to find somebody to talk to. Everybody was busy except Slim, who was sitting on the running board of his truck, strumming his ukulele, and singing a sad song about a train whistle, a letter, and a Birmingham jail. Jail! The very word tied Adam's stomach up in knots. Slim seemed to be matching Adam's mood, because he changed from a sad song to a lonesome one — "Red River Valley."

"I got a hankerin' to have me a little visit with them cows over there," Slim said when he finished the song. He motioned to where the animals were grazing a short distance away. "I'll take them a treat. Always keep barley in the truck — you never know when you might want to make friends with a horse or cow."

"I guess not," Adam muttered.

Sy was whistling as Adam made his way back to his camper, and he felt a catch in his throat. The tune was "Of All the Girls I've Loved Before." Had he ever loved a girl? He had admired from afar, but he was sure he had never really loved a girl, and he didn't love one now. And furthermore, he had enough problems to keep his mind in a frenzy and his stomach constricted for the next God knows how long. Thoughts of love had to be tossed aside.

Adam wedged a small piece of metal between the frame and the door on the storage compartment. That should make enough noise to waken him if he did doze off and someone opened the door. Then he spent a long time making a list of things he had to focus on. They included staying awake to listen for sounds, figuring out a way to pay the five thousand dollars if he had to because of the oil well escapade, searching for evidence that would help to exonerate him if he really was the main suspect in the fossil thefts, wracking his brain for clues as to who the real thief could be. But once he was in bed he couldn't keep his concentration on his problems. Visions of Jamie kept intruding. She was a strange mix — vivacious, foolhardy, definitely not the right girl for a serious-minded university student. He wasn't at university yet, but he tried to heed his mother's advice: *You can have anything you want if you want it badly enough. Visualize yourself being successful.*

Listen! Was that voices? No, just a calf bawling for its mother.

There would never be another Jamie. She was one of a kind — a wholesome, sensible girl-next-door with an adventurous streak. And she had smarts, too, plenty of them. She needed someone like him, actually, to tone her down when she went off on a tangent.

Five thousand dollars! How long would it take to save that much money? They wouldn't prosecute. They couldn't do that to a poor student.

He had to talk to Jamie before he left. He needed to know he could see her again. How could he worm his way into Devil's Coulee next summer? And what if he did worm his way in and she was somewhere else? And what if he was in jail by then? Next summer seemed an eternity away, but maybe he could ask her to write to him.

Adam rehearsed the things he might say. But she probably already had a boyfriend — his heart lurched at the thought.

Why hadn't he ditched the stolen stuff somewhere and forgotten about catching a scumbag thief?

Bring yourself back to your body, he told himself. *Breathe slowly and deeply. Keep things in perspective. It won't be the end of the world if you don't ever see Jamie again. Think about Hya and her pain.*

Hya's body decays. Her bones are slowly nudged away from her eggs by the forces of water and wind.

Volcanic ash makes the groundwater acidic and destroys most of the nests, but calcium carbonate helps neutralize the acid, and Hya's nest, along with several others, is preserved under many layers of silt from the seasonal flooding. As the sun and wind dry the soil, calcium carbonate forms around soil particles, and over a period of five thousand years or so, an entire layer of hardpan forms over the eggs. More floods, more silt, more hardpan — the eggs flatten under the weight.

Eons go by. The Bear Paw Sea drains away.

A one-kilometre-thick layer of ice grinds its way over the land. The sea levels drop and open a pathway from Asia to North America. The climate in Alaska and part of the Yukon becomes moderate. Corridors open through the glaciers.

The demise of the dinosaurs has allowed small mammals to proliferate, mutate, and evolve into more and more complex life forms. This unimaginably slow process has led finally to the biggest-brained creatures of all — Homo sapiens.

This new species of two-legged predators now masters the earth, and follows the game. For millennia humans struggle for survival in this harsh land.

Another change in climate causes the ice to melt and the oceans to rise, cutting North America off from Asia. As the ice age ends, causing flooding, many animals — *mammoths, mastodons, giant beavers, camels, and horses* — *become extinct. And so the cycle repeats itself. The ice comes, the ice goes. When the land is free of ice, vegetation grows, new animals flourish, and the two-legged creatures follow the food supply.*

They live in small groups of a dozen or so individuals, and one of these extended family groups of Paleo-Indians settles down and lives on top of Hya's nest. They do not know that their home was once her home.

Adam was halfway between waking and sleeping when he heard a sound. Footsteps! *Plonk! Plonk!* Pause. *Plonk!* He sat up with a jerk. More *plonks*, loud breathing. *Plonk!* Pause. How many of them were out there, anyway? *Snort!* That had sounded like horses. He had a sudden crazy vision of a band of bandits galloping around the countryside, stealing fossils right, left, and centre. Except there was no galloping, just plodding.

Cows! Huge, stupid, dim-witted cows.

The camper bounced and shook. *Bump! Rattle!* The mirror fell off the wall. *Bang!* A pot lid bounced off a shelf and clattered around the floor. The cows were rubbing against the camper's sides.

"Go away!" Adam whispered loudly, tapping on the window. More bumps and loud breathing. "You'll tip it over, for God's sake, with me in it. Go!" Adam pounded on the wall. "Go away." He banged his fists louder, and the animals stopped moving, but they didn't go away.

Adam yanked on his shoes, jumped out the door, and waved his arms. "Bug off!"

The cows didn't bug off. They stood and stared at him through half-closed eyes, then slowly moved a few steps and stopped.

Adam waited. The cows waited.

He grabbed the toy broom and waved it around. The animals lumbered off, but not far. They stood and gawked at the camper like a bunch of wide-eyed kids begging to go on a merry-go-round.

Adam spent the next ten minutes chasing cows with a toy broom.

He was crawling back into bed when he remembered the fake dinosaur egg. He leaped out, hurried around to the back, and wrenched the door open. It was gone! Adam cursed, sighed, and scuttled wearily back to bed.

CHAPTER 13

It was Saturday morning. Adam told Jamie about the cows and his failure as a night watchman. She said she understood perfectly and thought they should act normal and go ahead with their plan. What other options were there?

Denise, Lois, and Mike were getting ready to head off to Lethbridge in Al's Jeep with the cook driving. Lethbridge — where they could find ice cream and neighbourhood pubs with cold beer and shopping malls with movie theatres.

Herbie couldn't go. He had already left in his Volkswagen for Dinosaur Provincial Park. He was being "borrowed" because somebody had found what might be fossilized feces.

Slim had decided he was lonesome for his horses, Old Spike and Giddyup, so he had left in his truck to go and see them. Hans was going to work on notes for his thesis at the table in the cookhouse until noon and then planned to ride his bike to Sweetgrass in Montana just across the border from Coutts to visit the cousin of a friend who worked at the duty-free store there.

"She's a mountain biker, too," Hans told Adam and Jamie, "and I hear she's nuts about Canadian cheese, so I got a slab from the cook and a box of crackers to go with it." He patted the large pack attached to his bike.

So that was why he needed his laundry done, Adam thought. He was going to visit a girl. Hans was wearing a pastel striped sports shirt with a button-down collar, colour-matched grey pressed shorts, and socks that were whiter than white.

Sy was waiting to be picked up by on old oil well buddy from Warner who was going out to do some surveying. Al was working on the acid baths, now located in the specimen hut, and was waiting for the arrival of the museum curator.

"Are you sure you don't want to come to town?" Denise asked Jamie. "There's room for both you and Adam."

Jamie waved. "No thanks, Denise. Adam's never been to Writing-on-Stone. We're going to ride our bikes and take a picnic."

Bonnie passed, by wheeling her borrowed bicycle with the kangaroos riding in the front carrier.

"So you're heading to Writing-on-Stone to get pictures?" Jamie asked.

"That's right, sweetie. Looks like a perfect day for it."

"We're going there, too. Do you want to go with us?"

Bonnie shook her head. "That won't work. I have to write a letter and do some other stuff, so I won't be ready for an hour or so. You go ahead."

"Okay," Jamie said. She turned to Adam. "If we're going to do lunch, I'd better go and rustle up some grub, as Slim would say."

"Want me to help?" he asked.

"I can manage it."

Twenty minutes later Adam met Jamie at the fossil hut.

"Goodbye," Al said. "Have a good time and behave yourselves."

"Make up your mind, Dad," Jamie said with a grin as they shoved off. "The cook left cold chicken, homemade bread, and cheese for us," Jamie told Adam as they headed south toward the U.S. border.

"Sounds good," Adam said.

Jamie's scrubbed face seemed rosier than ever in the morning sunshine. She had the rosiest cheeks of any girl Adam had ever known, and he was beginning to think that rosy cheeks were very nice. Her eyebrows, showing above the top of her sunglasses, were shaped like feathered wings, arched in the centre, tapering to a fine line at the temple.

Adam was surprised to discover that the farther they got from camp the more distant and unimportant his worries became. In fact, he felt almost lighthearted for the first time in days.

"So what now?" he asked.

"We watch for suspects heading for the border. Hans, Sy, and Bonnie, I guess, or anybody for that matter."

"Silly of me, but I've always had this old-fashioned idea that you follow suspects from behind, not in front."

"Not necessarily." Jamie's eyes sparkled. "There's an old barn near the turnoff to the park."

Adam nodded. "An old barn. Well, isn't that something? I sure wouldn't want to miss seeing an old barn."

"How about hiding in one?" Jamie asked.

"Hiding? What do you mean?"

"We hide in the barn. Maybe Bonnie's meeting a guy and doesn't want to be seen. That would be the best place for a rendezvous for kilometres around."

"And if she's not meeting a guy?"

Jamie rolled her eyes. "She'll have to go past there no matter where she's heading. The road branches and goes in three directions. And we can watch out for Hans, too."

"Yeah, that cracker-and-cheese story sounded pretty phony to me."

"Exactly. And did you notice the way he was dressed? The perfect picture of a fine upstanding young man. Who would ever suspect him of smuggling?"

"So here we have two clever, quick-witted sleuths with a master plan," Adam said sarcastically. "We hide in a barn. We watch for Bonnie to ride by on a bicycle. Or not ride by on a bicycle. Or meet somebody. Or not meet somebody. Or stop at the barn. Or not stop at the barn. Or all of the above." He flung his arm out with a flourish. "And we watch for Hans to go by carrying crackers and cheese ... It's clear as mud, Jamie. I think you've been studying the chaos theory of the universe, because that's what this plan sounds like to me. Chaos with a capital *C*."

Jamie giggled. "Aw, Adam, lighten up. This is Saturday. We're supposed to be having fun. Is there anything else you'd rather be doing? It's an adventure, and we just might track down some fossil thieves."

"Believe me, Jamie, there's nothing else I'd rather be doing than chasing wild geese with you." He smacked a kiss in her direction.

"Don't forget, though. We want to get any little clues we possibly can. Maybe Sy's story about his oil well buddy is a front. Maybe we'll see him heading toward the border." Jamie grunted as they started to pedal up a hill. "When Hans comes along, we'll stop him and accidentally poke at his pack, or sort of lean on it and see if he looks worried. If we're suspicious, we can stop at a farmhouse and phone and warn them at the border crossing." She was panting in between words. "And we need licence numbers of vehicles, descriptions of anybody we see," she continued. They had reached the top of the hill and started to coast down. "Think serendipity. We might find something important when we're looking for something else. Keep an eye peeled for serendipity."

"Serendipity here we come," Adam said, waving his hand in greeting.

Near the border crossing at Coutts, a dirt road joined the paved one they had been on. Number 500 led to Writing-on-Stone Provincial Park, so the sign said. According to the map, this road, heading east, paralleled the Canada-U.S. border for approximately fifteen kilometres before making a sharp turn north.

They got off their bikes. Four mailboxes stood outside the fence on the southeast corner of the junction. Adam looked along the dirt road. "There's the barn where we can hide and wait for serendipity."

They headed for the barn, and a car appeared.

"A Montana licence plate," Adam said. "But if it's our fossil thieves, they've got the whole gang in there."

It was full of people. Five or six smiling faces and waving hands responded to Adam's and Jamie's salutes. The car's left-turn indicator started to flash, and the vehicle slowed for the stop sign, then turned onto the Coutts road, heading for the border.

"I'll write down the licence number, anyway," Jamie said, pulling a pencil stub from her pocket.

The old barn was about as typical of an old barn as one could imagine. There were rusting wagon wheels, old ploughshares, a grease-covered pump, and numerous empty cans and bottles of various shapes and sizes piled against the wall on the outside. An old hay rake, its row of curved tines half full of dusty straw, stood near the door.

"We can hide our bikes around the back," Jamie said.

They found a grassy spot in the shade beside the barn door where they were hidden from view, and yet could watch the junction where the roads met.

"I'll have a look inside," Adam said. He picked up a rusty spike and handed it to Jamie. "Tap with this if you see anything suspicious." He pointed at the skinny metal wheel of the rake.

Adam opened the door and stepped into semi-darkness. The windows were small and high, and any panes that hadn't been broken were thick with dirt and flyspecks. Broken shovels, a hole-riddled milk pail, and a ladder with two missing rungs stood against the wall. A row of metal stanchions hung at odd angles, open and forlorn. Adam felt a lump in his throat as he imagined the stanchions holding fat cows with full udders, chewing their cuds, switching their tails, waiting to be milked.

Was that the sound of metal on metal? He hurried to the door.

Jamie pointed. "Somebody on horseback."

The horseback rider stopped beside the mailboxes.

"Maybe I should go check him out," Adam said.

"Yeah, I think so," Jamie said.

"I don't want him to see me leaving the barn, so I'll bring my bike around and you give me a signal when he's not looking this way."

Adam rode the two hundred metres along the lane that led to the barn as fast as he could, then changed to a leisurely pace, scanning the scenery as he rode. He stopped when he reached the horse and rider. "Hi," he said. "Have you ever been to the park up that way?"

It wasn't a man. It was a woman. She was sitting with both legs on one side of a western-style saddle, one hand resting on the horn, the other on the cantle. It was hard to tell her age. She could have been anywhere between thirty and fifty. "No," she said. "But I hear tell the carvings are worth a look."

"Oh, good," Adam said. "How long would you say it would take to get there?"

"Dunno." The woman glanced at her watch. "Maybe an hour. Maybe less." She was wearing a cowboy hat pulled well down over her face, sunglasses, a long-sleeved light-weight cotton shirt, and jeans. The woman jumped down, led the horse into the ditch, and dropped the reins.

The horse was a small sorrel with a white patch on its face that resembled an upside-down violin. It started browsing on the grass. "Good boy, Skipper," the woman said, smacking its rump. She started to pace back and forth along the road, swinging her arms and breathing deeply. "You live around here?" she asked.

"No, I live in Calgary," Adam said.

"Just out on a visit?"

"You could say that. Actually, I take art lessons and I was heading for the park to do some sketches. But now that I see that barn there ..." He placed his thumbs and forefingers together to form a rectangle, held them up away from his eyes, and focused on the barn through the frame.

The woman stopped pacing. "Yeah, that would make a good picture."

Adam eyed a pack on the back of the saddle. "Looks like you're out for a long ride."

"Yep. They're having a cattle drive. You know, one of those 'down memory lane' things. They're calling it 'Hooves of History.' I'm heading for Cochrane to join in. Have to make a few overnight stops. One thing about cattle-drive people, they're friendly as all get-out. Lots of places I can bunk in. Think I'll have a rest here and a bite to eat." She settled herself on the grass near the horse.

Adam was beginning to feel anxious. Bonnie or Hans

could come along any minute. "Guess I'll go check the barn," he told her.

"Have fun."

Adam waved as he rode off. "Good luck with the cattle drive."

Jamie was still sitting where he had left her.

"No serendipity there," Adam said. "She's going to a cattle drive in Cochrane."

"Ditch your bike," Jamie said urgently. "Bonnie's coming."

Adam hurried around the barn, threw his bike down, and stood close to the wall. "Is she coming along here?"

"No," Jamie said. "She's just getting to the corner. The woman with the horse is still there. Bonnie's stopping. She's talking to the woman. Adam, come here!" Her whisper was urgent.

Adam hunkered down and ran the few steps to crouch beside Jamie.

Bonnie was beside her bicycle. The woman stood next to her horse. They seemed to be talking. Bonnie pulled something from her bicycle carrier and handed it to the woman. The equestrian stuffed the package into her pack, zipped it, jumped on the horse, and galloped along the dirt trail toward the west.

Jamie stared at the scene open-mouthed. "What's going on? You said she was going to Cochrane. That's not the way to Cochrane."

"Maybe this *is* serendipity," Adam said. "But what's it all about?"

Bonnie was back on her bicycle, riding along the road toward the barn.

"We better go in." Jamie grabbed his hand and pulled him inside.

They watched from the dim interior as Bonnie got closer.

"This is weird," Jamie said. "How come she gave something to that woman? It couldn't be fossils. Who would smuggle fossils out of the country with a horse?" Jamie's forehead was furrowed, and her eyes were almost closed.

"What if that's it?" Adam asked.

"What if what's it?"

"What if —"

"Shh!" Jamie put a hand over his mouth. "She's turning in here. Act as though we're getting real friendly. Look embarrassed." She put her arms around his neck and snuggled up. "Uh, hi, Bonnie." Jamie blushed and pushed herself away from Adam with such force that he almost lost his footing and took a step backward.

Bonnie stood motionless in the doorway, supporting her bike with one hand.

Adam's thoughts were racing like toy slot cars — and getting derailed like them. How can anyone *pretend* to blush? What had Bonnie given the woman? Why did Bonnie come to the barn? If Jamie really was blushing, what did that mean?

He pulled himself together with a start. He'd better *do* something instead of standing there like a dim-wit. "Where are Kanga and Roo?" he asked in a firm voice. "I thought you were going to take pictures of them."

The colour drained from Bonnie's face.

Jamie rushed to her and put a hand under her elbow. "Are you okay? Are you going to faint or what?"

Bonnie covered her face with her hands, shook her head, sobbed, and swayed.

"Adam, help!" Jamie said as Bonnie slumped to the floor. "Get water! And bring my sweatshirt."

By the time Adam had grabbed Jamie's sweatshirt from her bicycle rack, pulled a water canteen from the frame of his own bike, and returned, Bonnie's eyes were open.

Jamie lifted her head and tucked the folded shirt under it. "Here, drink." She yanked up the siphon from the canteen and put it between Bonnie's lips.

"I'm in terrible trouble," Bonnie said in a low voice. "You're going to hate me when I tell you."

"Aw, come on, Bonnie," Jamie said. "It can't be that bad."

Bonnie sat up shakily. "It is. It's worse than you think A lot worse. I … I … took stuff." Her voice was muffled as she leaned forward and buried her face in her arms. "And handed it over to be sold."

Jamie's voice was expressionless. "You took stuff?"

Bonnie shuddered and glanced at Jamie. "Fossils."

"But how did you hide them?" Jamie asked.

Bonnie began to cry. "Under Roo. In Kanga's pouch. I pulled out all the stuffing."

Adam grimaced. Under Roo. In Kanga's pouch. Of course.

"Bonnie, it's not the end of the world," Jamie said.

"It's the end of my world," Bonnie said between sobs.

"We have to do something and do it quick," Adam said. "I'll try to catch up to the woman and follow her. Find out where she's going."

Bonnie lifted a tear-stained face. "She'll be back. She has to drop Kanga and Roo beside the gate. For a refill. Oh, Adam. Be careful." She started to cry in earnest.

"You can't go alone," Jamie said.

"I can and I will," Adam insisted, heading for the door.

"No. We're in this together." Jamie started to follow him.

Adam turned and spoke sternly. "Listen to me, Jamie. I can go a lot faster by myself. You have to stay here with Bonnie."

Jamie sighed. "You're right. But be careful, Adam. Please be careful."

"You and Bonnie should go back to camp," he said. "If I don't return within two hours, call the police."

Jamie shook her head emphatically. "No way. I'm not leaving this barn until you get back here, so just forget it."

CHAPTER 14

Don't think. Ride. Concentrate on leg muscles. Send energy to the legs. Push. Push. Push. Push. Ride. Ride. Ride. Keep focused. Don't look around. Don't think. Just ride. Hard! Watch the road ahead.

The road was bumpy, full of potholes and ruts, and Adam was breathing hard and getting tired. He had been pedalling for a half-hour. Until now the road had been straight and he had been able to see ahead, watching for a woman on horseback. Now the road was becoming twisty, and there were shrubs and trees growing beside it.

He tried not to think, but a nasty fear began to creep into his consciousness. What if Jamie wasn't safe? What if Bonnie was putting on an act? She was very good at that. What if something horrible happened to Jamie while he was off trying to be the big hero? And Al had warned them to stay together!

Adam jammed on his brakes. Had he just passed a trail into the bush? The trail was well concealed from the road, but as he looked back he could see crushed weeds and grass. He would ride on a little farther, ditch his bike, and sneak back.

Ditching his bike wasn't hard. Sneaking back was. He moved among the trees as quietly as he could — saskatoon bushes, red osier dogwood, wild rose, chokecherry. None were very tall or dense. He reached an old track where the shrubs and grass had been recently flattened by large tires. Then he caught a glimpse of sunlight reflecting on metal.

Moving slowly toward the brightness, he heard voices and managed to get a few steps closer. He hardly dared to breathe. The horseback rider was talking to a man who was leaning against a battered old Cherokee truck. Behind it was a horse trailer. The rig must have been backed in. Pretty tricky driving.

Adam wasn't close enough to hear the conversation, but he did catch a few words.

The man's voice was urgent. "Bloody stuffed toys back ... Now! Get going! Meet you ..." Adam strained to hear, but the horse chose that precise second to swish its tail.

The woman jumped into the saddle. Her voice was a little louder "Yeah. Give me twenty minutes' head start."

Adam ducked behind a rose bush as the horse and rider passed within two metres of him.

He had to get close enough to the truck to see the licence number.

Adam gingerly took one step. Another. A third. He was partially hidden behind the trunk of a poplar and peered around it. The man was nowhere to be seen. The truck cab was empty. Nobody could have gotten into the horse trailer without opening the back gate, and he would have heard that.

The only sounds were the calls of birds, the chirp of crickets, and the buzz of grasshoppers. When he got close enough to see past the trailer, he caught a glimpse of the man in the distance, walking away along the rough trail.

Adam moved quickly and stood in front of the truck. It had an Idaho licence plate, and he memorized the numbers.

It wouldn't take them more than a half-hour to drive from here to the border at Coutts, and once into the States they could easily ditch the trailer and change the licence plates on the truck. Or ditch it, too. Maybe it was stolen. If only he could do something to immobilize it until he had time to get to a telephone. Stick a potato in the exhaust pipe? Where could he find a potato?

What else? Sugar in the gas tank? A dirty trick — it would ruin the engine, but all the better. He didn't have any sugar, though. Would anything else do? Waste of time thinking about that. The gas tank had a lock on it.

What else? What else? What else? His mind darted around like a crazed thing. *I've got it!* he almost spoke the words aloud. *Yank the ignition wire off the coil.* He darted along to the corner of the trailer and peeked around. Nobody. He raced back to the front of the truck. *Hurry! Hurry! Hurry!* He lifted the hood slowly and quietly, then stopped and listened, darting another quick look along the path. Still nobody. He had to do this fast!

Adam worked as swiftly as he could, but it wasn't fast enough.

A voice behind him demanded, "What do you think you're doing, sonny boy?"

Adam wheeled around.

The man stood six metres away, legs braced apart, head tipped back, and in his right hand he held a small gun — pointed at Adam's chest.

The realization hit like a ton of bricks. The trail must loop around and connect with itself closer to the road. That was how they had gotten the rig in with the trailer behind the truck! What a dim-wit he'd been.

"Uh, hi," Adam said. "I thought maybe the truck was broken down and I'd have a quick look under the hood." He tried to hide the quaver in his voice.

"Oh, you did, did you?" The man walked toward Adam, still pointing the gun. "You look familiar. In fact, I think we've almost been introduced." His voice was soft and threatening. "You work on that dinosaur dig, don't you, old buddy?"

Adam's skin crawled. He tried desperately to think of something to say, but what was there? This stranger seemed to know all about him.

The man wasn't familiar to Adam at all. He had a few day's stubble of dark beard, his eyes were hidden behind blue reflective sunglasses, he was wearing a baseball cap with a horse's head emblem on it, a western-style shirt gaping open between each set of snap fasteners, and new-looking blue jeans cinching in his torso under a large belly.

Adam tried to smile apologetically. "I'm sorry. I shouldn't have touched your truck."

"I just bet you're sorry. Yeah, I just bet you are. Especially since you got caught. I don't know what you were up to, but I'm sure it was dirty tricks. Come on, get going." He motioned with the gun toward the back of the trailer.

Adam turned, praying at every step that he wouldn't get a bullet in the back.

The man kept the gun trained on Adam while he fished a key from his shirt pocket with one hand and unlocked a padlock on the horse trailer door. He pulled it open. "Get in!"

Adam did as he was told.

"And if you try any funny business, you'll be dead meat," the man said as he closed the door.

Adam heard the padlock being snapped shut, and a few seconds later the truck door slammed and the engine roared into life.

Keep a cool head, he told himself. *Don't panic.* There had to be some way ... The trailer started to move. Adam sat on a horse blanket in the corner behind the driver's side of the truck and braced himself as well as he was able against double jeopardy — the bouncing up and down and the swaying from side to side.

The trailer held a sack of grain, two ropes hung on pegs, and a halter lying on the floor with its rope tied to a wooden bar. A wooden tool box holding curry combs, hoof clippers, tins of salve, a set of spurs, and other assorted horsey bits and pieces was strapped to the floor. That must have been where they carried the stolen fossils. Maybe it had a false bottom.

What a perfect ruse — the people at Customs and Immigration would be a lot more interested in the horse's credentials than anything else, and undoubtedly all the papers for it would be in perfect order.

The ride got smoother for about fifteen minutes and then Adam's heart skipped a beat as the vehicle slowed and stopped. They must be picking up the woman. And the horse. What would they do with him? Leave him in the trailer with the horse? Take him up into the cab with them? Or ... he tried not to think of the other alternative.

The door jerked open, and the woman with the horse stood there. Behind her was the man holding his gun.

"Stay right where you are!" the man ordered. "Get that horse into the trailer!" he barked at the woman.

The woman peered at Adam, then proceeded to do as she was told.

"Hi." Adam waved at her as she coaxed the horse in backward. "Didn't make it to Cochrane, eh?"

She glanced at him and then quickly away. She looked worried.

"Come on!" the man said impatiently. "Get the lead out!"

"But we can't take him," the woman protested. She was starting to loosen the cinch on the saddle.

"Don't be an idiot. Of course, we can't take him. And get out of there. You can unsaddle later."

"What are we going to do with him?" she asked as she tied the reins to a ring on the wall.

"We'll find a nice secluded spot, and then it's curtains!"

"No, you can't. He's an artist." The woman stepped down to the ground.

"I don't care if he's Michelangelo. He's got to go. Do you think we can waste all the time and money we spent on this job to have it wrecked by an idiot kid? Not to mention the years we spend rotting in jail when he blows the whistle on us? Don't be stupid."

"But they wouldn't have any way of tracking us —" The woman's words were interrupted by the slamming of the trailer door.

"I said it's curtains! The end! Can't you get that through your tiny little brain?" The man's loud voice was followed by the slamming of the truck door.

Adam shuddered. Curtains? The end for him? He would never again see Jamie or his family, never draw another dinosaur, never ride a bicycle. Even the sound of the truck engine seemed so precious that it made him want to cry. The smell of the horse was incredibly pungent and alive. He would never smell anything again. Tears brimmed in his eyes, and the lump in his throat hurt so badly that he was certain he would choke.

He had to be calm. Think of some plan, any plan, to try to save himself, no matter how wild or ridiculous it might seem. If only he had paid more attention to the martial arts part of his tai chi training.

The woman was on his side, but he didn't see how that could help. What could she do against a man with a gun?

Was there some way he could use the horse to help him escape? He glanced around. What if … could that possibly work? What if, when they stopped to get him out to do the ugly deed, he made the horse go wild and created a one-horse stampede? How? The spurs? Maybe. What if he jabbed the horse with a spur at precisely the right moment? Wouldn't it kick, lunge out of the trailer, run away, and cause so much commotion that he might be able to escape? Pretty crazy plan. And a pretty mean trick on the horse. He had to think of something else.

What if … what if he got *on* the horse? Just as they opened the door he could yell and kick the horse's flanks and the horse would jump out. He *might* be able to stay on a bucking horse. He had gone trail riding a few times when he was younger and knew enough to loosen the reins, say "Giddyup," and lean forward in the saddle to make it go. And he knew how to pull on the reins and say, "Whoa," to make it stop. But that was about it. Too crazy! There must be something else he could do.

But there was nothing else. It was his only chance. The road was bumpy again. It was coming! The secluded place where his body would be left to rot and would never be found.

Adam told himself to breathe slowly, calmly, and deeply.

He whispered to the horse, "Okay, Skipper, good boy." He untied the reins and patted the horse's neck. "It's all right, Skipper. Nothing to worry about. We can be friends." He climbed into the saddle and leaned forward as low as he could over the horse's mane. Now that he was up here he could see out the narrow space between roof and wall.

There were some trees around. If only they stopped soon, he might have a chance.

The vehicle slowed. Stopped. This was it! Adam's heart was racing, his hands were sweating, and his mouth was dry. The truck's engine died. The key grated in the padlock. *Ready?* The door opened. *"Giddyup!"* he yelled at the top of his lungs. He kicked his heels backward and lunged forward. The horse leaped out of the trailer almost throwing him over its head. He heard the sound of a gunshot. Adam tried to lean low over the horse's neck, but he bounced around like a stampede cowboy on a bucking bull. Both hands clutched the horn. *Hang on! Hang on!* His body rocked this way and that. The horse settled into a steady gallop, and it got a bit easier. He urged the horse on. *Faster. Faster.* He glanced behind and caught a glimpse of the man writhing on the ground. He heard loud voices yelling orders, cursing.

So far so good. Maybe the worst was over now. He sucked in huge gulps of air. What next? They would soon get the truck started and come after him, and though the horse was fast, it surely couldn't outrun a vehicle. He needed to watch for a likely spot to hide, then stop the horse, get off, and run. Adam was sure the man wouldn't be able to catch him on foot, especially if he had accidentally shot himself. The guy looked as if he was ready for a heart attack, anyway.

The horse continued to pound along, and Adam kept bouncing and watching the side of the road. The prairie was bald and wide. There were a few little hills and gullies, but no place to hide. He could hear the truck's engine now.

"Whoa!" He yanked on the reins. The horse stopped so suddenly he almost flew over its head again.

Drop the reins. Jump. Run. Run. Run like crazy. Run like a rabbit. Run like a cheetah. He stampeded into a gully, then up and over a hill and across a bare, gravelly patch of ground, through some silver sage, and across a meadow of wheat grass. He was sure his lungs would burst. *Run! Run!* He scrambled over a dry creek bed and scuttled toward a bed of buckbrush, flinging himself flat on his stomach and crawling under the sprawling branches as well as he was able to. He lay still. He figured he was making more noise than the truck with his gasping breath and pounding heart.

Adam pulled aside some upward-twisting limbs and peeked through. He couldn't see the road, but he could make out the top of the trailer. It was standing still. Should he make another dash for it? Get farther away from the road and take the chance of being seen? Or should he stay where he was and hope he was well enough hidden to escape notice? Better to stay and calm down. He didn't think the small gun the man had would shoot very far, and he would be able to see anybody coming across the field for at least three hundred metres. He waited, then heard the engine start. He saw the top of the trailer move, then disappear.

Adam wanted desperately to get up. His ribs were sore, and the sticky evergreen leaves of the buckbrush were stinging his forearm like fire ants. How come? He looked at his arm and saw for the first time that he had scraped it badly. When? He couldn't think. He started to stand, then flopped down again. What if it was a trick? Maybe they were pretending to leave so he'd show himself.

He watched for what seemed an eternity, twisting his forearm up and hoping a little breeze would cool it. A ground squirrel poked its head out of a hole and stared at him with black inquisitive eyes. A coyote loped past not six metres away, stopped, turned its head to study him, stood motionless, then ran noiselessly in the other direction.

Adam sniffed. Was that alcohol he smelled? It seemed to be coming from a bush. It was. He must have scraped the bark of a skunk bush in his dive for cover.

He glanced at his watch. It was 2:40. He had been lying here for over an hour. He would chance it. He stood and looked toward the road. All was still and quiet. But which way should he go? He didn't dare go back to the road. He didn't know where he was. Which way should he walk?

Adam was thirsty and thought longingly of the second water bottle attached to his bicycle frame. *Water!* Hadn't he jumped a dry creek bed a short distance away? And didn't creeks always lead to rivers and didn't rivers always lead to civilization? Sure, the creek was dry now, but it must run sometime. Toward a river. Too tired to run, he walked quickly, found the creek bed, and started to follow it.

The vegetation along the dry creek was different — wild raspberry, water birch, chokecherry, and thorny buffalo berry, so he took shortcuts, at least he hoped they were shortcuts, keeping the creek bed in view.

His ribs were getting sorer by the minute, and he supported them with his arms as he walked. His mouth was parched. He would give anything for a drink of water. Anything.

He imagined he heard running water. *Wait a minute!* It wasn't his imagination. He *could* hear running water. And smell it. He reached the edge of a plateau and looked down. The Milk River seventeen metres below glistened whitish in the late-afternoon sun. He followed the river for a short time, and suddenly he stopped. He must be hallucinating. That looked like pavement ahead.

CHAPTER 15

It was a parking lot, with cars and recreational vehicles parked in marked spaces. A sign with a pointing arrow indicated TOURIST INFORMATION CENTRE. Adam hurried along, past a cabin with a PARK WARDEN sign on the gate.

Another sign said TOILETS. Toilets meant water! Usually. Maybe these were dry. He rushed toward a small building set in the trees. It was dry. He would ask a tourist for a drink, if he could find one. There didn't seem to be any people around, only vehicles.

Adam spotted a telephone booth at almost exactly the same instant that he spied a drinking fountain. Fantastic! He was the luckiest person alive. Two prayers answered at once.

The first few slurps of water were lukewarm, but it soon got cooler, and he sucked it in noisily, putting his mouth right over the spout, something his mother had always told him he shouldn't do. Water. Delicious, wet, cool, heavenly water. He heard voices and paused to look up. A group of people were coming through a gate where a fence marked some kind of boundary.

A young woman wearing a Parks Branch uniform approached. "Hi, there. I'm sorry, but the last tour is finished for the day." She looked him up and down.

"That's okay. I don't want a tour. I just want to use that telephone."

"Did you fall or something? You look a bit smashed up."

"Not exactly," Adam said. "It's a long story. I got lost and followed the river, and — what park is this?"

"Writing-on-Stone. Do you need a ride somewhere?" People were climbing into vehicles and starting their engines.

"Well, I might. Thanks. Can I phone first?"

"Sure. Go ahead. Where are you heading?"

"Devil's Coulee — the dinosaur dig," Adam said as he hurried to the phone booth. Now that he was about to phone, the anxiety about Jamie washed over him again. What if something had happened to her? "Operator, I'd like to place a collect call." When the connection was made, he was surprised to hear Jamie's voice. "Adam!" She blew out a loud breath. "Thank God! Are you okay?"

Adam's skin crawled with goose bumps at the sound of her voice. She must have gone back to the dig with Bonnie. He was so relieved that he felt like doing sixty somersaults and the highland fling. "I'm fine. Are you?"

"Yeah. Where are you?"

"Listen. First call the police. Tell them to look for a Cherokee four-wheel drive pulling a horse trailer. Idaho licence." He gave the number. "They probably went through the border at Coutts a couple of hours ago."

"Got it. Where are you?"

"Writing-on-Stone."

"*Writing on Stone?*" Her voice sounded incredulous. "How did you get there? Oh, never mind. Everybody's out looking for you. They found your bike. They keep calling to see if I've heard anything. We better get off the line. Just stay there. Don't budge."

"Wait!" Adam cried. "The guy driving the truck could be hurt. He might go to a hospital or clinic for help."

"Got it," Jamie said. "Stay right there!"

Adam hung up the phone and walked slowly toward a bench. "Thanks," he said to the tour guide. "Somebody will be here to pick me up. I'll just wait." He sat down.

"Sure. Would you like something — chips or a chocolate bar? The snack bar is closed for the day, but I could unlock it."

"No. Thanks just the same." He didn't feel hungry, though he hadn't eaten anything since breakfast.

He sat on the bench, stretched his legs, and tried to figure out where he hurt most. His ribs ached with every deep breath. The scrape on his arm was deeper than he'd thought. It was embedded with caked blood and dirt. He had noticed a stinging sensation on his shin, and now he investigated. There was a lump the size of an egg under his sock.

Adam wished vaguely that he had enough energy to look around. The tourist display board would probably have information about what kinds of drawings were on the stones, but he was too tired and sore. He stretched out flat on the bench.

"You sure you'll be all right?" The tour guide was back, dangling a set of car keys.

"Yeah. Thanks a lot. They'll be here any minute." Adam raised a hand and gave a limp wave. "Pardon me for not getting up."

"No problem. You look like you've had quite a day. Losing your way in these badlands is no laughing matter," she said sympathetically. "I think I'll just wait until your ride comes." She sat on a bench adjoining the one Adam was using. "You said the dinosaur dig? You work on it?"

"Yeah." Adam tried unsuccessfully to stifle a yawn.

"Oh, sorry. I guess you don't feel like talking."

"No, no, I'm the one who's sorry. It's just that I've had a long day." And a terrifying one, he added to himself. He didn't want to think about that just now. He had come within a hair's breadth of dying with a bullet in his brain, and he was alive. Alive and lying on a bench surrounded by peaceful hills and ancient rocks. Rocks that had been lovingly carved and painted centuries before by human beings who had felt compelled to leave their stories for future generations to read. About their gods, their rituals, their dreams, their enemies, love and despair, life and death. The whole thing was just too much to contemplate at the moment.

Adam didn't have to contemplate the whole thing until two hours later. By that time he'd had a careful shower, his scrapes had been cleaned and bandaged by Al and Jamie, he'd eaten six slices of toast with peanut butter, one apple and two bananas, and he'd drunk a quart of milk. A roast beef dinner with Yorkshire pudding and gravy and apple pie for dessert couldn't have tasted better.

He was sitting at a picnic table with Jamie and Al. The evening was calm and still — sweet with prairie smells. The cool air gently pushed away the heat of the day.

"So tell us exactly what happened from the moment you left Jamie and Bonnie in the barn," Al said.

Adam told them, answering questions when he forgot details, repeating himself in some parts, stumbling over his words when he talked about the most frightening moments.

Jamie was silent, watching him wide-eyed, nodding, looking horrified at times, smiling at others.

"Well, son, that makes you quite a hero," Al said. "It was a reckless thing to do, but it's had a happy ending — so far."

"Yeah, so far," Jamie said. She looked alarmed. "What if those guys come after Adam? They know where he is."

Adam shuddered. It was possible, definitely possible, but he had to convince himself that it wouldn't happen. It couldn't happen.

"They won't." He waved his hand. "What good would it do them now? They've already been fingered. Your dad says the police have an all-points bulletin out for them. They'd be crazy to come across the border looking for me."

Jamie leaned forward and put her hand on his. "But, Adam, you're the only one who can identify them." Her eyes were wide with fear. "They could get a hired gun." She looked panic-stricken at the thought.

"Jamie, lighten up," Adam said. "The odds that those thugs are going to do a hired-gun thing are practically zilch. I'm a nobody from nowhere. Anyway, I can't live in fear." He patted her hand.

"I think we're getting ahead of ourselves," Al said. "We haven't heard Bonnie's story yet. I guess Jamie has heard some of it, but I need to hear it from Bonnie herself. Are you too tired to talk any more tonight?"

"No," Adam said. "I don't think I could sleep right now, anyway. I still can't understand how Bonnie could have done it."

Bonnie herself didn't seem to understand how she could have done it. Jamie had gone to get her, and they were now in the Jamiesons' trailer. At Al's insistence Adam was lying on a padded bench. Jamie and Bonnie sat on the bench opposite, and Al was sitting on a stool beside them.

Bonnie's lower lip trembled. "I was going to have to quit school. No money. This guy hung around the university, and

I guess he heard me telling somebody I had a chance to work on this dig, but it wasn't going to do me much good because I couldn't afford to go back for my last year, anyway."

"Shall I light a candle?" Al asked. Dusk was turning to darkness.

"No," Bonnie said. "Please. I like it like this."

"So he made you an offer your couldn't refuse?" Adam asked, then wished he hadn't. That was a dumb thing to say to somebody who was in a state of mental anguish. But Bonnie seemed to think it was okay.

"That's it exactly." She looked at him. "I was desperate. So far I'd gotten by with scholarships and bursaries, but my marks weren't high enough this semester, so …" She clenched her hands. "And the fees went up. Out of sight. There was no way, just no way. And I wanted to finish so badly, and all my family, and my parents. It's going to kill my dad when I tell him I've messed up, that I've *stolen* things." She hugged herself and started to rock back and forth.

"How many more fossils do you have to turn over before they'll be satisfied," Al asked.

Bonnie laughed bitterly. "That stuff I handed over was just peanuts. To prove my good faith. The real payoff is for information."

"Information about what?"

"About the exact location of the dig — with maps and everything. They're planning some kind of a big operation after the dig closes for the summer. I think maybe with dynamite and a helicopter."

"*Whe-e-e-w!*" Jamie whistled. "This is big-time all right. All the more reason they have to catch them." She brushed her hands together and plopped them on her knee as though the job were already done.

"Hey, I just thought of something!" Adam said. "The guy in the truck seemed to recognize me. Knew I worked on the dig. I'm sure I've never seen him before, though."

"Oh, no, it was the pictures," Bonnie said.

Adam frowned. "Pictures?"

"Remember all those pictures I took of everybody — the camp and the dig and everything?" Bonnie's voice was shaking.

Al's face darkened. "You handed them over to the smugglers?"

Bonnie put her hands over her face and nodded.

"So you not only stole fossils, you may also have jeopardized the lives of every single person on this crew!" It was the first time Adam had heard Al sound angry.

Bonnie began to cry.

Adam reached for a box of Kleenex on the window shelf and passed it to her. She yanked out three tissues without looking up.

"I just wanted to get enough money to go back to school." She sobbed and sniffled. "But once I started I got in deeper and deeper. There was no turning back." She hiccuped, gasped, and blew her nose. "They gave me an advance, and it got used up getting here. They'll go after my whole family if I double-cross them." She was crying so hard that the words came out in gasping whispers. "My little sister, Susie. She's only … only, six." Bonnie's shoulders heaved, and she wiped her eyes. Wadding the Kleenex into a ball, she clenched it in one hand and reached for more. "Susie's got big brown eyes. She loves to play in the park. She calls all the trees p-p-populars. We'll find her at the bottom of a river if I don't cooperate."

Jamie's voice was firm and reassuring. "It's okay, Bonnie.

You didn't know what you were getting into. At least not how bad it would be." She put an arm around her.

"It's not okay!" Bonnie cried. "It's dirty, rotten, dishonest, lying, cheating, thieving — all the things I could never have imagined I'd ever, ever do. Never in my life." She leaned down until her forehead touched her knees.

Bonnie didn't sound like Bonnie. She hadn't once said "sweetie" since she'd arrived.

"We'll help you," Jamie said. "Won't we, Adam? We have to keep this thing in perspective. The worst that's happened so far is that some old bones and one fake dinosaur egg are missing. Adam's amber and my teeth don't count for much."

"Yeah, you're right," Adam said. "And now that we know all about their master plan, we can nip it in the bud."

Al cleared his throat. "It may not be necessary to worry about the master plan. If they catch those two, there's a good possibility we'll get the stolen goods back, and I think the police should have a pretty good chance of finding the ring-leaders. I have high hopes they will, with all the information Adam's given us. Things may turn out for the better, Bonnie girl. I'll testify for you if it comes to a court case."

Bonnie lifted her head and gazed at each one of them through tear-filled eyes. "You mean you don't think I'm the scum of the earth? You mean you'll try to help me?" Her voice was shaky, and the expression on her face changed slowly from one of disbelief to a small glimmer of hope. "Thank you, Al. Thanks, Jamie. Thanks, Adam." She reached for one hand after another as she spoke. "I don't deserve it, but thanks."

She stood and smiled wanly. "This is the first time I've felt half-decent for two months. I made a big mistake, and I'm going to do everything I can to pay the penalty and rejoin the human race, if I get a chance."

"We've got a guard on the gate, so you can sleep in peace," Al said as Bonnie started to leave.

"Thanks, Al," Bonnie said. "You're a good guy."

"By the way," Jamie said, jumping down after her, "I almost forgot to ask. Did you leave a pile of berries under a tree in the saskatoon patch?"

"Yeah," Bonnie said. "I hid the fossils in the pail when I first grabbed them, just temporarily, and I needed extra berries to cover them up. I figured nobody would think of searching through a pail of saskatoons."

"Or a kangaroo's pouch," Jamie added. She turned back to the trailer door. "I'll walk you to your camper, Adam."

Sitting up was an ordeal in itself. Sharp intense pain grabbed Adam's ribs when he tried to lift his upper body weight. He rolled carefully onto his side, let his legs hang over the edge of the bunk, then pushed with his hands until he was in a sitting position.

Al was watching. "We'll get you to a doctor in the morning."

Adam shook his head. "No. It's just cracked ribs. I've had them before. They hurt like the devil, but they get better themselves."

"Okay, son. Good night. Hope you get a decent sleep. You've had one heck of a day. Here, take these for the pain." Al handed Adam a small plastic bottle containing several white pills. "The instructions are on the label."

As Jamie and Adam walked to the camper, the stars were so bright and low that it seemed as if you could reach up and pick them.

"I'm so glad you're okay, Adam," Jamie said. "I was worried sick about you."

"No more than I was about you," he said, looking at her. The whites of her eyes were clear and bright in her shadowy face. Her irises were almost as dark as the black pupils, except when a moonbeam reflected a flash of turquoise.

"Why were your worried about me?" she asked.

"After I left you with Bonnie, I had this horrible thought that maybe you were in danger. That somehow Bonnie might pull a dirty trick."

"She was in no condition to try to pull anything. Poor Bonnie. I do feel sorry for her." Jamie shook her head, and the nut-brown and auburn cascade of her hair, and the flash of her teeth between slightly parted lips, made Adam's heart skip a beat.

He cleared his throat. "Jamie?"

"Uh-huh?"

He stared at the sky. "I wish I could come back next year."

Jamie's reaction was immediate. "Oh, yeah, yeah. I've got that all figured out."

Adam swallowed. "You have?"

"Yeah. They're working on some new displays at the Royal Tyrrell Museum, and I mentioned to Dad that you'd be a good bet to help paint the dioramas."

"Paint dioramas? At the museum?" Adam tried to keep his voice from showing his disappointment. He took a deep breath. "That's not exactly what I had in mind. I was sort of hoping I could get in on the dig again here." He paused. "Can I ask you something?"

"Ask away."

"Do you think I'm stodgy?"

"Stodgy? What do you mean?"

"Well, when you first went out on a limb to get me in

here, you said you wanted somebody your own age who wasn't stodgy, but I'm afraid stodginess is in my bones."

She smiled. "Adam, are you trying to tell me something?" She tilted her head back and squinted at him through half-closed eyes.

Adam was overwhelmed with feelings of embarrassment and inadequacy. His hands hung limply at his sides. His face was hot and his skin prickled. He had been kidding himself. He had never been any good with girls and he never would be. He wished he'd kept his mouth shut and gone quietly back to his camper like a sensible person.

"Look at me, Adam," she said. "Now what is it you'd like to tell me? I know you'd rather draw than talk, but talk to me. In words." She put her hand lightly on his wrist.

The feel of her hands, the smell of honeysuckle, the hum of insects, and the distant strumming of Slim's ukulele made it seem easy.

He took a deep breath. "Jamie, I've never met anybody like you ..." But it wasn't easy, after all. What did he really want to say to her? It was simple. He wanted to tell her that he wanted very badly to see her again, and ask her if she felt the same way. But he was terrified. It was very much like the feeling he'd had the first time he'd rappelled over a cliff edge. Do it fast, don't think about it, just take the plunge.

He took the plunge. "I was hoping I could get to see you again next summer, if not sooner." There. The words were out, but he didn't dare look at her.

"Like, yeah. I was hoping that, too," she said.

"You were?" Adam had always thought he could never again feel the thrill of that first rappelling jump, but he'd thought wrong. This was like *wow!* Like *zing!* Like the world had just changed colour. Like all the birds were singing in unison. Like he was rappelling over a whole range of mountains. "You mean it? You're not just saying that?"

She laughed and leaned toward him. Her eyes sparkled and her hair spilled over her shoulders. "Do I usually say things I don't mean?"

"No."

Later Adam lay on his bunk and savoured the euphoria. He was still alive after being so close to dying. And Jamie wanted to see him again. Jamie would persuade her father to let him come back to the dig next year. Jamie would write him letters — at least one a month.

CHAPTER 16

By the time Adam had finished packing his bag the next morning, there was good news.

"They got them," Al called as Adam headed toward the fossil hut.

"Really?" Adam would have jumped for joy if jumping had been in his repertoire, but the best he could do at the moment was grab Al's hand with his left one. "What a relief!"

"Yes. You were right about the guy having a gunshot wound. He went into a medical clinic, and they nabbed them both. The police think that a plea bargain will lead them to the big guns. You deserve a medal, son." Al supported Adam's left elbow with one hand and shook his hand warmly with the other.

Herbie was back, and he was excited. They had found the real thing, fossilized droppings, probably from a *Chasmosaurus* — the horned one.

"How are you feeling?" he asked Adam. "Hear you had quite an ordeal."

"Yeah, but I'm fine," Adam said. "Couldn't be better." That wasn't exactly true. His ribs hurt worse than ever, his leg was stiff, and bruises were beginning to show on his thighs.

"And how's Bonnie?" Herbie asked. "I feel sorry for her. I can understand how it can happen. Finishing up that final term can seem more important than anything else in the world after you've spent three-quarters of your life getting that far."

"She's packing up to leave," Adam said.

Herbie looked alarmed. "She's not going home, is she?"

"No. Not right now. She's going to stay with a relative somewhere for a while."

"How's she getting to the airport?" Herbie asked anxiously.

"Slim's dropping her off on the way to Calgary for supplies. He's giving me a ride home, too."

"I wouldn't mind taking her," Herbie said. "I'd like to talk to her. A guy I know is writing a thesis on international law. I'm sure he'd like to interview her, if she's willing." He headed toward Bonnie's tent.

Mike, Lois, the cook, and Denise left for a local stampede at Taber, calling Adam a "hero" and "our mighty man" as they waved goodbye. Hans had telephoned to say he wouldn't be back until Monday morning. The cheese had been a big hit with his friend's cousin, and believe it or not, her mountain bike was a dead ringer for his own. The two of them were going riding and camping together.

"Sounds like the love bug has bitten our Hans," Al said with a grin. "By the way, I'd like to take a look at some of those drawings before you leave."

"Well," Adam said, "it just so happens that I kept my sketchbook out hoping you'd ask. They aren't that great, but I'm sure I can do better with practice." He handed them over.

Al studied them. "Hmm. They're pretty close. The proportions aren't *quite* right. Tell you what I'll do. I'll have somebody at the Tyrrell mail you some diagrams of skeletons and pictures of models. You definitely have talent there, son. Send me a portfolio after you've done a little more work."

"I sure will, Al! Thanks for everything. You've been … um, I think you're one of the best guys ever. See you next summer, I hope." Adam shook hands with Al again and then went to look for Jamie.

He felt a little pang of anxiety as he passed Sy's camper and heard him whistling "Of All the Girls I've Loved Before." Would things be the same between Jamie and him in the morning sunshine as they had been in the evening starlight?

Jamie was hanging laundry on a rope clothesline behind the Jamiesons' trailer. Her hands danced in the sunlight as she shook out a white shirt, held the two shirttail ends in one hand, reached up for a clothes peg, deftly pinned one side, then the other. It was like a ballet the way she did it.

"Hi." Adam didn't know what else to say. The same old feelings, the ones he thought he'd conquered, came over him as he looked at her. He was a zero with women. It had just been the magic of the moment that had carried them away the evening before. She would tell him now that she'd been mistaken, that it was just a flash in the pan. Then she would say goodbye.

"Guess what, Adam?" she said.

His heart lurched.

"I found out why Sy never takes his hat off." She seemed larger than life as she walked toward him.

"You what?" Adam tried to collect his wits.

"I found out why Sy never takes his hat off." She tilted

her head back and studied him smugly.

"Why?"

"He's bald."

"Bald?"

"Like, yeah, he's bald." She nodded several times.

"How did you find out?"

"He was in the shower this morning and …" She paused.

"And you grabbed his hat and hid it?"

"No-o-o-o." She smiled. "I would never do a thing like that."

"Oh?" Adam raised his eyebrows.

"Uh-huh. He was adjusting his hat as he came out and I saw his head."

Adam whistled. "Well, I'll be jiggered, as Sy himself would say. So that solves the mystery of the Panama hat."

"Yep, and I guess that just leaves one thing for us to talk about."

"Just one …" Adam said. "So let's talk about it, okay?"

"Like, sure. The dig has been the best ever because I met you and we had a lot of fun. But every time I think about poachers I get so mad I could spit!"

"Exactly, it's rotten. We did what we could to get them, but I guess there are a lot more of them out there waiting in the wings." Adam stared into the distance. "You know, we should try to invent something, some way to protect fossils, video cameras in balloons or something." He turned his head to look at her.

Jamie took his left hand in both of hers. "Do you think it would hurt your ribs if I give you a little hug?"

Adam shook his head numbly.

Jamie carefully put her arms around his shoulders and snuggled her head against his neck. "I'll miss you," she whispered.

"Me, too." Adam put his left arm around her.

Jamie drew in a long, ragged breath and pulled away. "Did I hurt your ribs?"

He smoothed the hair back from her forehead. "To heck with my ribs!"

"I hope you'll still want to come back next year."

"Oh, I will, I will. Volcanoes and earthquakes couldn't keep me away."

"Even if you can't come back to the dig, don't worry," she said. "We'll figure out something."

Right on, Adam thought. Probably something risky, illegal, or downright dangerous. Maybe all three. He could hardly wait.

"Yeah, well, like, goodbye." Jamie brushed the blossom of a wild geranium with the toe of her boot. "Hey, maybe you could come to Drumheller at Christmas. We could cross-country ski."

"That would be terrific," Adam said. "But I'll probably have to work."

She looked disappointed.

"But I'll try, for sure. Even a couple of days."

Jamie brightened up. "Yeah, but if you come, don't you dare ride that bike. Take the bus."

She was being bossy again, but now it sounded fine. Like concern for his well-being rather than actual bossiness.

"This is it for now then." She turned back to the clothesline. "Do you mind if I don't come to see you off?"

"No, that's okay. Goodbye. Don't forget to write."

As he was walking away, he turned to look back at her. She held the clothesline with one hand and blew him a kiss with the other.

The year is 1987. A female high school student wanders the badlands of the Milk River Ridge as she has done since she was a child, prospecting for fossils. She picks up a small fragment of something she recognizes — an egg shell. The young woman gives the specimen to a university professor, who passes it on to the curator of the Royal Tyrrell Museum. The hunt is on.

For three weeks the team searches, covering hundreds of kilometres of ground. Finally, the young woman takes the others to a favourite childhood haunt called Devil's Coulee, so-called because its shape resembles the Devil's pitchfork. It is a three-pronged ravine that scars the prairie grassland. Through it wind badlands, carved out at the end of the last ice age by swift-flowing torrents of melting ice water.

The young woman goes to write a mathematics exam.

It is a hot afternoon. This is the last day for prospecting this year. No luck. The crew packs up, ready to call it quits. One man has not returned for the rendezvous.

He is sitting down for a rest on the side of a hill nearby. He glances down. Small bones stick out of the sandstone near his feet. He brushes the earth away and sees the fragmentary outline of an egg. He jumps up. More bones. Higher up the hill there are bits of egg shell, then he spies part of an egg with ribs sticking out of it. He runs, yelling, to the others. They hurry back to the hill.

By the time the mathematics exam is finished, the men are as happy as the Paleo-Indians who found the new land.

The hillside is littered with baby dinosaur bones, sections of eggs, even articulated bones protruding from an exploded egg.

They reach the top of the ridge. Although they do not know how many, they do realize that dinosaur nests are buried in hardpan at different levels beneath their feet. In the top level, only three feet down, is Hya's nest. It will soon be excavated with meticulous care.

Her bones, lying on the hillside, have eroded out into sunshine two hundred metres away. Her never-to-be-born babies will be studied and revered by hundreds of thousands of creatures who could not have been here if she and the rest of her species had not died.

These creatures know that this was once her home.